THE
HAUNTING
OF JESSOP
RISE

Also by Danny Weston:

The Piper
Mr Sparks

THE
HAUNTING
OF JESSOP
RISE

DANNY WESTON

ANDERSEN PRESS • LONDON

First published in 2016 by
Andersen Press Limited
20 Vauxhall Bridge Road
London SW1V 2SA
www.andersenpress.co.uk

2 4 6 8 10 9 7 5 3 1

ISBN 978 1 78344 461 8

MIX
Paper from
responsible sources
FSC® C018072

Printed and bound in Great Britain by Clays Limited,
Bungay, Suffolk, NR35 1ED

To Keith and Jean Saunders –
great friends, always.

PART ONE
OCTOBER 1853

CHAPTER ONE
THE LONG WALK

William crested the hill and paused for a moment to look down into the bay. It was a blustery night and the ocean moved restlessly beneath a full moon, rushing back and forth onto a wide shingle beach. Even at this height, he could hear the rhythmic swishing of water on stone far below him. Off to his left, set back from the sea and arranged on a distant hilltop, was a circle of tall standing stones, stark in the moonlight, their grey shapes casting long shadows on the ground. Away to his right, he had his first clear view of what must be Jessop Rise. It was perched high on the cliff edge, a big, crumbling ruin of a place, stark against tumbled moonlit clouds, and it seemed to be positioned here so the occupants could gaze out across the sea for mile after mile. To a boy who had only ever seen the ocean at a distance, it was a powerful moment.

William adjusted the bundle on his back, which contained everything he had in the world, and considered the fact that he had been walking solidly for the best part of four days. His ankles were rubbed raw by his heavy boots, and the soles of his feet were blistered and aching. He'd spent every night of his travels sleeping in barns and outbuildings, sneaking into them after dark and leaving well before the sun was up. The only food he'd had over this time were the berries and roots he'd foraged along the way and the occasional meagre offerings from people he'd met as he travelled, kindly souls who despite being poor themselves had taken pity on this young boy, out on his own.

He didn't know Wales at all, even though it was the land of his birth. But coming back here was certainly preferable to staying on at the workhouse in Northwich, surviving on the awful food and dealing with the endless bullying of the older boys. He told himself that however unfamiliar his uncle's house was, it had to be an improvement on what he had endured over the past few months.

William started along the clifftop track, the powerful wind gusting in off the sea threatening to blow him off his feet at any moment. As he walked, he thought of Mrs Selby's face when she'd called him into her study, five days ago.

She was the person charged with the day-to-day running of the workhouse, a heavy-set, scowling fright of a woman, with a face that looked as though she were being forced to swallow something that tasted bad. She'd glared at him as he stood in front of her desk, his cap in his hands, his head bowed.

'Well, boy,' she said, 'it would appear that all your prayers have been answered.'

He stared at her, mystified. 'My...prayers?' he echoed.

She lifted a sheet of writing paper from the desk and waved it at him. 'I have a letter here from a Mr Seth Jessop...'

'Who?' William couldn't help himself. It was his own surname, sure enough, but the Christian name meant nothing to him.

Mrs Selby grimaced. 'Your uncle,' she elaborated.

He continued to stare at her in bemusement.

'Your dead father's brother?' she added, saying it slowly as though speaking to an idiot. 'Oh, come along, boy, you must know of him. He lives in North Wales, does he not?'

William shrugged. 'I think I do remember my father mentioning that he had a brother,' he murmured. 'He told me he had fallen out with his family years ago; he had very little to do with them.'

'Yes, well, he must have a forgiving nature, your uncle. At any rate, he's offered to give you a home.' She looked positively outraged at this news. 'He wants to take you off my hands, just as the two of us were beginning to get acquainted.' She glanced slyly at the willow cane hanging on the wall above her desk, a cane that William had already learned she was more than happy to use on any boy who incurred her wrath – something that was surprisingly easy to do. You only needed to be a little bit slow in following one of her orders. 'Well, don't just stand there gaping like a stranded fish,' she told him. 'Aren't you pleased? Aren't you delighted?'

William nodded, but he was still utterly mystified. 'Excuse me, Mrs Selby, but how...how did my uncle even *know* about me?'

'The authorities must have written to him, I suppose. Informed him of your father's untimely death and reminded him that, as your next of kin, he had a moral duty to offer you some sort of help. I imagine they expected nothing more than a few guineas in financial assistance, but he's actually offered to give you a home in one of the finest houses in North Wales.' She laughed at the sheer improbability of it and pushed the letter across the desk to him. 'Here, read it for yourself,' she suggested. She thought for a moment. 'You *can* read, I take it?'

'Yes, Mrs Selby. I...I was going to school before my father...' He found he couldn't continue down that line. It made him think about the accident and of his father, lying pale and drawn in a hospital bed, gasping for breath as death placed its cold hands upon him, so he busied himself looking at the letter. It was short and to the point.

Jessop Rise
Porthmadog
North Wales

Dear Mrs Selby

I was deeply saddened to hear of my brother's recent demise and of my nephew's resulting predicament. As somebody who has himself suffered at the hands of tragedy, I can fully appreciate the boy's plight and I cannot in all decency allow him to remain a ward of the state.

Luckily I am in a position to offer the boy a roof over his head and three square meals a day. Please tell him to come to my home at his earliest convenience and I shall find something useful for him to do.

Yours sincerely

Seth Jessop Esquire

The message was so brief that William found himself turning the paper over to see if there was anything else written on the back of it, but that was all. He placed it back on Mrs Selby's desk and looked at her.

'Wales?' he said.

She gave him an impatient look. 'What about it?' she snapped.

'I know nothing of it.'

'But your late father was a Welshman, was he not?'

'Yes, ma'am, but...we came to Northwich when I was just a baby.'

Mrs Selby shrugged. 'I cannot do much about that, can I? Think of this as an opportunity to reacquaint yourself with your homeland.'

'Yes, ma'am. Excuse me, ma'am, how...how will I even *get* there?'

'That,' said Mrs Selby, 'is entirely up to you, boy. But you will leave these premises at first light tomorrow, so we can offer your bunk to somebody less privileged than you. We won't be short of applicants, of that you can be sure.'

So at first light the following day, he'd done as she suggested. He had no idea how far it was or how long it would take him to reach his destination. As it turned out it was a journey of over eighty miles, and the workhouse had given him nothing for the trip but the clothes he stood up in, an old blanket, a crust of dry bread and a tattered map that Mrs Selby had found for him. William was glad that he had it as he made his way steadily south-west, through Kelsall, Chester, Ruthin and a whole collection of towns that he couldn't even pronounce, until finally he reached the very end of the country, beneath the spot where the long arm of North Wales pointed out into the sea. The armpit, William decided, looking at the map.

And now here he was, in a place where the land ended abruptly, falling away to the moonlit sea far below him. He turned and followed an ancient track towards the old house. The path rose and fell, the dirt worn smooth by the passage of generations of feet. It switched this way and that, dropping steeply into unexpected declivities and then rearing up again so that William was sometimes obliged to balance on slippery rocks, uncomfortably aware of how close he was to the sheer drop at his left. One slip and that would be the end of him, he realised, so he stepped with great care. Gradually he grew closer and closer to Jessop Rise. Every muscle in his body protested at this last trudge, but he steeled himself and kept on going, telling himself that food and drink would surely be waiting for him when he finally reached his destination.

He was perhaps no more than half a mile from the house when he came to a place where a high rocky outcrop edged the track to his right and he became aware of a figure, sitting on the rocks a short distance ahead. As he drew closer he saw that it was a woman, her slight frame cloaked and hooded against the rough winds that flapped and shook the folds of the loose grey garment. A small lantern at her side bathed her body in a weak yellow light, but somehow failed to illuminate her face, which was lost in the shadow of her hood. William decided that she was gazing towards Jessop Rise, as though watching it intently. She made no sign of being aware of his presence; she just sat and stared in the direction of the house. As he came alongside her, he felt compelled to stop and speak. In such a desolate place, it would have seemed rude not to say something.

'Good evening, ma'am,' he said, trying to push aside the exhaustion that made even talking an effort. He pointed towards the house. 'Would that be Jessop Rise?' he asked.

She made no effort to reply, just kept gazing fixedly at it.

He wondered if perhaps she had failed to hear him, so he tried again, raising his voice to shout over the blustering wind. 'Excuse me, ma'am. Am I...am I heading along the right path to...?'

His voice trailed away as her head turned in his direction. He still had no impression of a face contained within the hood, just a dark hollow that seemed as deep as a pit. The sight of it seemed to momentarily still his blood in his veins. He swallowed hard, aware that the woman's eyes must be studying him with the same intensity with which they had watched the house. He felt compelled to say something more.

'It...it is my...my uncle's house. Seth Jessop. He has invited me to...'

But then the head turned away and went back to studying the distant building, as though the woman had dismissed him.

'Well,' he said, and he was aware of a tremor in his voice as he spoke. 'I'll b-bid you goodnight then.'

He resumed walking quickly onwards and had taken perhaps three steps when he distinctly heard a hoarse voice behind him: 'Good night, boy,' followed by a breathy laugh.

Fear rippled through him, and despite his tiredness he quickened his pace, almost tripping and falling on an outcrop of stone, but he managed to steady himself. When he had walked another twenty paces or so, he paused to glance back and felt another thrill of apprehension when he saw that the stone outcrop was now completely empty. He looked this way and that, trying to work out where she could have gone, and it occurred to him that she might have left her perch in order to follow him. The thought of that lent him wings. He kept on going and did not slow his pace again until he reached the gateway of the house.

CHAPTER TWO
THE HOUSE ON THE CLIFF

There was a stone archway at the top of the path with the name of the dwelling inscribed upon it in an ornate script. William noticed that the word 'Jessop', unlike the word 'Rise', looked rather amateurishly carved, and more deeply inscribed as though whatever had been there before had been chiselled away and the new name added by a less skilled craftsman. William pushed open the metal gate and walked up the wide driveway to the front door, his feet crunching on gravel. It was only now he was up close that he was able to fully appreciate the sheer size of the house. It towered above him, three storeys high, a great dark edifice of grey stone, its black windows staring blindly down at this puny newcomer as if challenging him to come closer. He got the impression that the house was very old, that it had stood here for generations, watching its inhabitants come and go.

William climbed the flight of lichen-encrusted steps to the front door. A length of metal chain hung alongside it so he reached out and gave it a tug. A bell clanged somewhere deep in the bowels of the house and he waited, wondering how late it was. Perhaps everybody had gone to bed. After a short while, however, the door creaked slowly open and a woman's face peered out at him: a haggard, disapproving face with ragged black eyebrows and a thin downturned mouth, above which the faint outline of a moustache was evident. She was holding an oil lamp, the dim light giving her lined features a distinctly ominous look.

She said something then, or rather she growled it in a language he didn't understand and he stared back at her helplessly. 'I'm sorry,' he said. 'I don't—'

'I asked you what you want at this time of the night!' snapped the woman, in a strong Welsh accent. 'What's the matter with you, boy? Don't you speak God's own language? I took you for a local lad.' She sounded to be in bad humour.

'If you please, ma'am, I'm...I'm here to s-see my uncle Seth,' stammered William. 'I believe he's expecting me.'

'Is he indeed? Well, he hasn't said anything to me about it.' Her eyes narrowed. 'You're saying that you're a Jessop?' she asked incredulously. 'Mr Jessop's nephew?'

He nodded. 'Yes, ma'am,' he said.

The woman seemed astounded by this information. 'Wait yure,' she said, and the door slammed shut in William's face. He stood on the step for what seemed a very long time. Growing bored of waiting, he turned and looked back along the drive to the stone arch. Beyond it lay the rugged stretch of the clifftop, framed against that restless sky. This seemed such a remote place, so different from the narrow bustling streets of Northwich where he had grown up. There was a terrible sense of loneliness here, the feeling that whoever chose to live in such a house was shunning the rest of the world. This was a place for people who liked their own company.

William turned back as the door creaked open again and the same woman looked sullenly out at him.

'It seems you *are* expected,' she muttered, as though she had anticipated being told otherwise. 'Why nobody ever bothers to inform me of such happenings is a mystery to me.' She sighed. 'Well, I suppose you'd better come inside,' she added. 'And make sure you wipe those boots before you go stepping on my clean floors.'

'Yes, ma'am.' William did as he was told and found himself in a large, dimly lit hallway. He could see the woman better now. She was short and dumpy, wearing an odd frilly white cap and a shapeless black dress. A thick woollen shawl hung around her shoulders. She watched in silence as he wiped his boots on the doormat until she was satisfied that they were spotless.

'I am Mrs Craddock,' she told him. 'The housekeeper at "the Rise". Mr Jessop has just told me that I'm to treat you like everyone else yure and that you're to do as I tell you. Is that clear?'

'Yes, ma'am,' said William.

'Good. This way.' He followed the bobbing light of her lantern along a narrow hallway. He had a fleeting impression of large paintings on the walls to either side of him and they passed a tall mirror, which briefly reflected the glow of the lamp in all directions. Then Mrs Craddock pushed open a door and ushered William into what appeared to be a large dining room. He was expecting her to follow him in, but she closed the door behind him and he found himself standing facing the room's occupants, a man and a youth, who were sitting at a huge table, eating by lantern light. A generous log fire blazing in a marble hearth added to the light in the room, and William noticed that there were two large, scruffy wolfhounds stretched out in front of it. The room stank of their cloying, musky odour.

William returned his gaze to the diners. The man was a lithe, muscular-looking fellow with straight black hair, centre-parted and hanging to his shoulders. He studied William with keen dark eyes as the boy approached the table. His craggy face was ruggedly handsome, dominated by a long, sharp nose, but his chin was covered by thick stubble and his clothes looked grubby as though they hadn't been changed in a long time. The other diner was perhaps only a few years older than William, heavy-set with pale, chubby features under a thatch of unruly blond hair. He was much more smartly dressed than his companion. His eyes too appraised William, but without much interest. The youth seemed far more concerned with his supper.

The man took a chicken leg from a serving dish and took a huge bite from the flesh, an action that made William's empty stomach lurch. The man chewed noisily, studying William the whole time. Then he wiped his mouth on the sleeve of his jacket and flung the remains of the drumstick across the room to the dogs. It was snatched up by the nearest of them and devoured in one noisy snap.

'So,' said the man, 'you're here at last.' The strong Welsh accent reminded William of the way his father used to speak, but unlike him, this man's demeanour was cold and aloof.

His lips curled upwards into an unpleasant sneer. 'I was expecting you *days* ago. What took you so long?'

William was taken aback by the question and it took him a moment to find the words to frame an answer. Finally he managed to reply.

'Sir, I...I had to walk.'

'From Northwich?' The man seemed to find this incredibly amusing. He leaned back his head and laughed at the very idea of it. 'But that's more than eighty miles! Did nobody at the workhouse think to supply you with the coach fare?'

William shook his head. 'No, sir, they did not.'

'Who would believe it?' He waved a hand. 'Well, no matter, you're here now and that's the main thing. Mrs Craddock tells me you don't have any Welsh. Is that right?'

'It is, sir,' said William. 'I'm sorry, sir.'

'And you born not a stone's throw from here! That's a sorry state of affairs, isn't it?'

'Well, you see, sir, my father never—'

Uncle Seth waved a hand. 'It's of no consequence,' he said. 'We all speak English here. I am married to an Englishwoman, you see. That hulking specimen sitting beside me is my stepson, Toby. He can barely string a sentence together in the local tongue, though I've tried hard enough to teach him.' The blond boy grunted but said nothing, so the man continued. 'Half of the workforce up at the quarry are from Liverpool or Manchester, and if you tried speaking Welsh to them you'd get some pretty blank looks in return. The way things are going, the language will be dead and gone within fifty years.' He shrugged, as if to indicate that it wouldn't take much skin off his nose if that happened. 'I expect you're exhausted,' he said. He noticed the intensity with which William was studying the plates of food on the table and added, 'Hungry too, I'll wager. Well, come along, boy – don't stand on ceremony. As you can see, we do not bother with etiquette here.' He indicated an empty chair beside him. 'Sit down, grab a plate, help yourself to some food.'

William needed no second bidding. Within moments he had thrown down his bundle and was tucking into a large sausage and a hunk of bread. The man watched him for a moment in apparent amusement. 'See how you're wolfing that down!' he exclaimed. 'When did you last eat?'

'Two days ago,' said William, through a mouthful of bread and sausage. 'A woman on the road gave me a piece of mutton pie.'

'Hear that, Toby?' the man asked. 'Two days without food! I'd like to see you go that long without taking sustenance. Two hours would be your limit!'

Toby grunted again as if to suggest that he didn't much care what the man thought and helped himself to a pork chop from a heaped platter in front of him. The man grinned and turned back to William. 'As you have no doubt realised, I am your uncle Seth.'

'I'm very pleased to meet you,' said William. He held out a hand to shake, but Seth ignored the gesture.

'We have met before,' he said.

'Er...really?'

'Oh, it was a very long time ago. Of course you won't remember it.' He pointed his knife at William. 'So you are Matthew's lad. You have the look of him, I'd say, in as much as I can remember him. How old are you, boy?'

'I'm fourteen, sir.'

Seth nodded. 'Four years younger than Toby here,' he observed. He looked again at his stepson, though his expression showed no sign of pride. If anything, he seemed irritated. 'Well, come along, lad, have you nothing to say to your poor orphaned cousin?'

Toby looked up from his plate with evident reluctance and

deigned to throw a look in William's direction. 'Hullo,' he said.

William nodded back, but for the moment was too eager to swallow mouthfuls of that succulent meat to make anything in the way of conversation. He reached out and grabbed another sausage from the platter.

Seth looked from one to the other of them, amused by their silence. 'Yes, well, hopefully you'll feel more like conversation when your bellies are full,' he observed. He lifted a glass of wine and took a generous swallow, then studied William again, as if wondering what to say next. 'So, Matthew is dead,' he said, setting the glass down, and the way he said it made William stop eating. There was no tone of regret in the voice. If anything, it sounded almost as though he was gloating. 'I understand there was some kind of...an accident?'

William swallowed hard. 'Yes, sir,' he said. 'He...he was crushed by machinery. At the cotton mill where he worked.'

Seth nodded. 'Oh, now there's bad luck. But...I was under the impression that he was a foreman there?'

'He *was*, sir. He...he was trying to help another man who was caught up in the same equipment. They...both died.'

Seth shook his head. 'That's doubly unfortunate. What's the point of being a foreman if you're going to wade in with the underlings? Mind you, he always was the sentimental sort, your father.' He stared at William intently. 'Tell me, boy, was it quick? Or did he . . . linger?'

William put down the hunk of bread he'd been holding. He could feel fresh tears coming and his voice wavered as he struggled to hold them at bay. 'He . . . he lasted two days in the hospital,' he murmured. 'He fought with everything he had, but . . . his chest was crushed, you see, and . . .' William's voice gave out and he wept, uncomfortably aware that the two of them were watching him with unwholesome interest. After a few moments he lifted an arm and wiped at his eyes with the sleeve of his coat. 'I'm sorry,' he said, as though he had done something wrong.

'Don't trouble yourself,' said Seth, waving a hand. 'Of course it's upsetting. You're an orphan now, what with your mother gone all those years ago. You must have been only a few years old when that happened.'

William nodded silently.

'Cholera, wasn't it? Ah well, that's what comes of living in towns, you see. They are not healthy places. Breeding grounds for germs and contagion.' He sighed, shrugging his shoulders. 'I knew your mother, William. When we were young, Sian and I were ... close friends. But then of course your father romanced her and eventually married her. He always seemed to take the things that I wanted.' He looked distracted for a moment as though remembering. 'And a year or so later he whisked her off to Northwich to start their new life together.' He smiled, but his eyes seemed to flash with resentment. 'Mind you, I know all about loss. My poor sweet Audrina – Toby's mother – has been gone just a little more than a year.'

He pointed towards the fireplace with a knife, indicating a large oil painting that hung above the mantle. It was the portrait of a lady, a thin, aristocratic-looking woman with intense blue eyes, her long fair hair elegantly braided and hanging onto her shoulders. She was smiling, but her expression was not really one of happiness, William thought. She looked uneasy, brooding, as though she had not felt comfortable sitting for the portrait.

'I'm sorry to hear it,' said William. He felt puzzled. Hadn't Uncle Seth just told him that he was still married? 'What ... what happened to her?'

Uncle Seth gave him a strange look. 'Nobody's entirely sure,' he said. He gave an odd little smile and then seemed to make an effort to change the subject. 'I wonder, William, do you remember your grandfather at all?' He pointed to another painting on the opposite wall. This depicted a fierce-looking old man with white hair and a bristling moustache. He was dressed in black clothes and glared down as though he resented the diners being here.

William shook his head. 'I'm afraid not,' he said.

'Well, why would you? You would have been no more than two or three years old when you last set eyes upon him. But I distinctly remember how he made such a great fuss of you! Of course, this was long before I met Audrina. I had no prospect of marriage then, and here was your father, the older brother, already married and with a young son to show off. The old man could barely contain his pride.' He scowled. 'Of course, he always favoured Matthew over me.'

'I . . . I didn't know that,' said William.

'Oh yes, absolutely! There was quite a rivalry between us, if I'm honest. Ever since we were little boys. It quite broke the old man's heart when your father decided to head to England to pursue his interests in King Cotton. Our father wanted him to take over the slate quarry, where the Jessops have always prospered. He thought me far too headstrong for the role.'

'Oh, I'm sure that—'

'Don't interrupt, boy.' Seth looked momentarily annoyed, but seemed to make an attempt to shrug his bad humour off. 'I remember very clearly Matthew's last visit to see my father,' he continued. 'The old man made him an offer that day: ownership of the family business, something that would have made him a wealthy man, but one that he politely declined.' Seth shook his head as though he still couldn't quite believe it, even after all this time. 'But that was Matthew for you. Proud, independent...beholden to no man.' Uncle Seth took another mouthful of wine, gulping it noisily. 'I stayed put of course and bided my time. I knew that persistence would eventually pay off, and this proved to be the case. The old man finally saw sense and made *me* his heir. When he became too infirm to continue, I inherited the quarry and then, of course, I met Audrina and married into her family, acquiring Toby as my stepson. And I came to live here in the Ransome family home. Even brought your grandfather here towards the end of his life, so he could live out the rest of his days like a proper gentleman. Now look at me! I'm the most prosperous man in the county.'

He chuckled, as though amused by his own good fortune.

'And, you know, your father could have had it all on a plate.' He tapped his own platter with the tip of a knife as if to emphasise the point. 'He could have owned the quarry. He could have had me at his beck and call. He only had to say the word. But no, he preferred to follow his own course, and look where that ambition led him. To a slow and painful death on a factory floor, while I . . .' He reached out a hand and plucked a plum from a bowl in front of him. 'I have everything that could have been his. Including, it would seem, his son.'

The remark was so spiteful it made William flinch.

Seth lifted the plum to his mouth and chewed thoughtfully for a moment, before spitting the stone onto his plate. Then he studied William again. 'So, now you are finally here, what are we to do with you?' he asked.

'*Do* with me?'

'"The devil makes work for idle hands." I'm sure you've heard that expression. And you do not strike me as an idle boy. After all, you've just walked eighty miles!'

'Would I . . . be able to resume my studies?' asked William, recovering himself.

Uncle Seth smirked. 'Your *studies*?'

'Yes, I was attending school in Northwich, before . . . before Father . . .'

Seth shook his head. 'Oh, we haven't much respect for book-learning in these parts,' he said. He glanced at his stepson. 'What do I always say, Toby?'

Toby recited the words as though he had been made to learn them by heart. 'Life is the keenest teacher,' he said tonelessly.

'Well remembered.' Seth looked sharply at William. 'And, you'll want to earn your keep, won't you?'

'Er...well, I...'

'I have been thinking of late that there's something Toby is in sore need of: a valet.' At this Toby looked up, appearing interested for the first time.

'A...valet, sir?' asked William.

'Yes. You know what that is, don't you? Somebody to tend to him, help him to dress, wash, fetch his things and generally pick up after him. Well, he's a young gentlemen now, and when he comes of age he'll be the heir to a considerable fortune. Of course, I could appoint a professional to the task, but wouldn't it be so much nicer if it were somebody in the family line? Somebody he could actually be *friends* with. So when I heard about Matthew's death, I thought to myself, why not let his son enjoy the privilege?'

'But, sir, I . . . I have no experience of—'

'Well then, look at this as a perfect opportunity to learn a new set of skills!' Seth spread his hands. 'And when all is said and done, how difficult can it be? There's no better training than first-hand experience. You shall make a start in the morning.'

'Oh, but . . .'

Uncle Seth's expression hardened. 'I feel sure you'll prefer living here to whatever it was you got up to at the workhouse. You'll have decent meals and a warm, dry place to sleep. Who knows, if you do well, you may actually come to enjoy the work.'

'But you see, I—'

'The only other option I could offer you is to work down in the slate quarry . . . oh, but that's a hard slog for a young lad. Back-breaking work it is – you'd be old before your time.' He seemed to think for a moment. 'I suppose there is one other possibility . . .'

William leaned forward slightly. 'What's that?' he asked.

'If you feel that the post of valet to my stepson is . . . *beneath* you, then you could always return to Mrs Selby and tell her that things haven't worked out between us . . .'

Seth smiled with exaggerated innocence and William realised he had little choice but to agree to his uncle's terms.

'Yes, sir,' he said. 'Of course, I'll do my best. Thank you, sir.'

'That's all settled then.' Seth leaned back in his seat and smiled contentedly. 'Well,' he said, 'I expect you must be feeling tired after your long journey. Toby –' he snapped his gaze sideways – 'if you've quite finished stuffing your face with food, perhaps you'd like to take young William here and show him where he'll be sleeping? Just for tonight you can wait on him, and from tomorrow it shall be the other way around.'

'Can't Mrs Craddock take him?' complained Toby.

'No, she cannot,' growled Uncle Seth. 'You'll do it with a glad heart or I'll box your ears for you.'

Toby was still chewing on what was left of the chop, but when he realised that his stepfather was glaring at him, he gave a weary sigh and flung the bone to the dogs. Once again it was wolfed down by the nearest of them with a loud snap. Toby wiped his hands and mouth on a linen napkin and got to his feet.

'This way,' he said wearily.

William would have liked to eat some more, but Seth seemed to have dismissed him, so he stood up from the table, collected his bundle and followed his cousin obediently out of the room.

CHAPTER THREE
AND SO TO BED

In the hallway, Toby picked up an oil lamp from a sideboard. He led William to a rather grand wooden staircase and started climbing it. William was obliged to follow close on his cousin's heels in order to stay within range of the meagre glow.

'You really walked all that way?' asked Toby, without turning his head. William could hear now that Seth had been right; there was no trace of a Welsh accent in Toby's voice. 'You actually walked for eighty miles?'

William tried not to sound surprised. 'Yes,' he said. 'It took me the best part of five days.'

'Only an idiot would walk that far,' observed Toby. 'An idiot or a pauper.'

'Well, there was no other choice,' William told him. 'I had no money.'

'What? Did your father not leave you *anything*?'

'I don't know. Any cash there might have been went to the workhouse for my upkeep. Mrs Selby would have made short work of that.' William didn't like to dwell on such miserable things. 'How...how long have you lived here?' he asked.

'All my life,' said Toby. 'Worse luck.'

'Why do you say that?' asked William. 'It is a fine-looking house.'

'Oh, I suppose so. In better days it was a good place to be. Of course, in my childhood it was called "Ransome Rise". That was the surname of my real father, who died when I was little. He was an English cavalry officer and he died in action, fighting for his country in India.' Toby made an action with one hand as though stabbing an invisible opponent with a sword. They reached the top of the staircase and turned right along the first-floor landing.

'So if your family is English, how do you come to be living here?'

Toby looked irritated. 'The Ransomes have *always* owned land in Wales,' he said. 'The estate was originally given to my great-grandfather for services to the throne.'

'And...now it is called Jessop Rise, because my uncle married your mother?'

'Yes, when I was around your age. Of course Seth wanted the house to be in his name, and he soon got his way.' He scowled. 'He always gets his way in the end. That's something you'll quickly learn about him. So now it is called Jessop Rise, and since my mother is gone, the two of us live here together. We've learned to tolerate each other.'

'And I suppose Uncle Seth works overseeing the quarry?'

Toby sniggered as though the very idea was a joke. 'He doesn't *work*,' he said. 'He has people to do that for him. Oh, once a month he has to pay them of course. Or at least he has to be present when the wages are handed out. It's expected. Lately he's been making me attend too. He says I should get used to the practice if I'm to be in charge here, when he's gone.' Toby paused and turned to look at William. 'So what do you think of the idea of being my lackey?'

William frowned. 'I . . . don't really know what to think,' he said. 'I wasn't expecting anything like that.'

Toby grinned. 'It's really quite simple,' he said. 'Provided you do as you're told, we shall get along famously.' He was still smiling, but something flashed in his blue eyes, something that had no hint of humour in it at all. 'Let me warn you, cousin: cross me, and you shall regret it. I'm a decent enough sort, but I do not suffer fools gladly.'

He turned away and started up the next staircase. Once again William had to hurry after him for fear of being left in the dark. They reached the second landing and turned to walk along it. William was beginning to appreciate just how big the old house was. It occurred to him now that he could have fitted his father's little rented garret in Northwich into the dining room of this place.

'Uncle Seth must be prosperous,' he observed.

'I think the term is "rich",' said Toby bluntly. 'And, yes, he's done rather well for himself. As if the proceeds from the quarry weren't enough, he had the good sense to marry my mother, who was the wealthiest widow in the county. Of course Seth will tell you that it had no bearing on his wanting to marry her, but...there are few people around these parts who would take his word for *that*.'

William was shocked to hear Toby talking about his mother and stepfather in such a callous manner, but Toby carried on speaking as if he had said nothing out of place. 'Actually it will be good to have some company around here,' he said. 'There's nothing much to do in this godforsaken wilderness, and a lad could die for want of some decent conversation. We don't see a new face from one week to the next.'

A third flight of stairs awaited them. 'Your room is up here,' said Toby. 'In the servant's quarters. You'll have Mrs Craddock next door to you.' He smiled maliciously. 'I'll warn you now, she snores like an old grampus. When she's in full flow, you can hear it all over the house.' They went quickly up the final set of stairs and Toby led William along the landing. The walls were bare plaster up here, and it was markedly colder than the lower floors. At the very end Toby pushed open a plain wooden door. William followed him inside. 'You'll sleep in here,' announced Toby, looking around with a grim smile. William followed his gaze and his heart sank.

They were in a bare, grubby room under the eaves of the roof. The ceilings slanted at forty-five degrees, lined with cobweb-strewn beams, and the only window was a dusty little dormer that looked out onto pitch darkness. There was a mattress on the floorboards in one corner on which a verminous-looking blanket was spread. Beside it, on a rickety table, stood a single candle in a tin holder and a box of phosphorous matches. Under the table there was an earthenware chamberpot. Toby went over to the table, set down his lantern and lit the candle. He stared at the flame as it blossomed into life and then gazed slowly around.

'Well, Seth has certainly spared no expense on you,' he said. 'I expect you must feel honoured.'

William shrugged. The room wasn't much of an improvement on the bunk he'd slept on at the workhouse, but at least it looked as though he would have the place to himself and, exhausted as he was, he didn't think he'd have much trouble getting off to sleep. He carried his bundle over to the mattress.

'I hope you don't mind my asking,' he said, 'but... what happened to your mother? Uncle Seth said something odd – that nobody was really sure.'

Toby turned to look at him, his face strange in the candlelight. 'What he meant was... she disappeared.'

'What do you mean?' asked William. 'Disappeared?'

'What do you suppose I mean?' snapped Toby. 'Come along, cousin. I appreciate you're tired, but you must try to concentrate.'

'Er... I...'

'She went missing. Seth was away at the time, on business, and I was laid up with a wretched fever. My mother went off for a walk one evening and... she never returned. There was no sign of her anywhere. She left no note, told nobody where she was going. She simply vanished.'

'Did they...look for her?'

'Of course they did! There was a countywide search. But no trace of her was ever found.'

'That's strange,' murmured William.

'It's worse than strange,' said Toby, looking suddenly haunted. 'You are left with the feeling that she could turn up again at any moment. For the first few months I lived in hope that she'd return and everything would go back to the way it was before. But now I fear the worst. I'm not wishing her dead, you understand, but at least if I could see her body, I'd know that all hope was gone.'

William swallowed hard. 'I saw my father dead in the hospital,' he whispered. 'I shall not forget that in a long time. He looked to be at peace, but...' He was aware that he was in danger of weeping again, so he made an effort to push the image from his mind. 'So...what do you think happened to your mother?'

'Who can say?' Toby looked at his hands. 'She and I were very close,' he said, 'and I'm sure she would not have left without a word to me. Not unless she was...compelled to go.'

'Compelled? You mean...?'

'That she was kidnapped. I've read of such things in my

detective novels. When that happens, the culprits usually send a letter demanding money. But there's been nothing.' He shook his head. 'Of course, there's been plenty of speculation about it around these parts. Some people think that she must have lost her mind and thrown herself off the cliffs. But I do not believe that for a moment. My mother was perfectly sane, of that I am sure. Others maintain that she had grown heartily sick of her marriage to my stepfather and so she went to live in another country. Oh, if you ask around in the village you're sure to hear plenty of opinions!'

'Why would she be sick of the marriage? Was it not a happy one?'

Toby shrugged. 'Who knows? They used to argue a lot, but I'm told that's the usual way of things in a marriage.'

'My parents never—'

'Some thought from the beginning that it was a bad match. It's no secret that my mother's own family did not approve.'

'Really?'

'Oh yes. They thought Seth far too rough in his ways for a woman of her breeding. Your family came from nothing, you understand, grubbing a living out of the rock, whereas my mother was from excellent stock. But she was stubborn, you see. She didn't care about convention. She stood by Seth, married him even though her own parents – my grandparents – refused to attend the wedding.'

'That must have been ... difficult.'

'Very. But she didn't care. She was besotted with him.' He must have caught a look of disbelief from William, because he added, 'He was very handsome back then, and he dressed like a gentleman. I think my mother's disappearance has taken a terrible toll on him.' He sighed. 'At any rate, Seth could make my mother do just about anything to please him ... even changing the name of the house.'

'So that's why the sign on the gate looked so odd,' murmured William. 'Somebody's chiselled out the old name and put the new one in.'

'Exactly,' said Toby. 'He had that done within days of arriving here.'

William frowned. A thought was nagging at him and he felt he had to mention it. 'Toby, you don't think ...? I mean ... if your mother and Uncle Seth were arguing, perhaps ...'

'I know what you are going to say,' said Toby. 'But the matter was fully investigated by no less than the chief law officer of the county, who announced that Seth had a cast-iron alibi. He was miles away when it happened, discussing business matters with an important client, a man who was happy to vouch for him. And besides, he doted on my mother every bit as much as she doted on him. Yes, they had arguments, but who doesn't?'

'Well, I...'

'And where's the motive? Do you really think if he'd murdered my mother for her thousands, he'd be living the life of a pauper out here in the middle of nowhere? Of course not! He'd be a rake, spending money at the gaming tables, going off to society functions... why, if I thought for one moment he might have had anything to do with my mother's disappearance, well...' He shook his head and glanced sullenly around the room. 'So, we rattle along, the two of us,' he said. 'I hate it here, without her. It used to be such a friendly place. Now it's cold and boring. I've been reading about what's happening in the Americas and in Australia and it makes me yearn for new horizons. Perhaps your father had the right idea, moving to England. I imagine that in Northwich you at least saw other people from time to time.'

William thought of his school back in the town, the earnest children sitting at their wooden desks, doing their studies, while the schoolmaster chalked his lessons up on the blackboard. He missed that more than he could ever have imagined he would. He had just been starting to realise what a big and promising place the world was and how he might fit himself into it. 'It *is* remote here,' he admitted.

'It is more than remote,' snarled Toby. 'It is desolate. Aside from the workers who bring food and firewood, the only other people who ever call at this house are from the quarry: agitators complaining about the poor conditions. I imagine they have a point, but they get short shrift from Seth, I'll tell you that much. If he had his way, they'd eat fresh air and work every hour the good Lord sends.'

'What about your grandparents? Do you not see them?'

Toby snorted. 'They wouldn't come here if you paid them,' he said. 'And Seth does not encourage me to visit *them*. He feels they're a bad influence on me. He says they *spoil* me. I miss them terribly.' He sighed. 'I cannot tell you the last time I saw a new face around here. Apart from yours, of course.'

William thought for a moment. 'I passed somebody on the way here,' he said. 'As I came along the cliff path.'

Toby laughed scornfully. 'Oh, I doubt that,' he said. 'Nobody ventures along that old track, especially at night.'

'But I did see somebody. A woman. All wrapped up in a cloak.'

'What are you talking about?' snapped Toby. The colour had suddenly drained from his face.

'Oh, it was...just a person that I passed. She was sitting on some rocks. I thought it strange because it looked as though she was watching the...'

William broke off as Toby laughed derisively at him. 'Who've you been talking to?' he demanded. 'I would have expected more of you, cousin! Oh, if you choose to listen to the locals with their superstitious tales of witches and demons, no wonder you've started seeing things!'

'But, cousin, I...I haven't been speaking to *anyone*, I assure you! I have only just arrived. And I tell you, I saw a woman...'

Toby took a threatening step closer and raised his hand, as if to strike William. 'I'm warning you,' he said. 'If you say another word on the subject, I shall not hold back. Do you hear me?'

William raised his own hands in a gesture of submission and Toby lowered his arm, his face like thunder.

'I don't understand,' said William. 'I only—'

'Let us get something straight between us,' said Toby.

'I do not believe in such nonsense. I *will* not believe it!' He paced for a moment, clearly agitated. Then he stopped and looked at William. 'People have, on occasion, tried to tell me that they have seen my mother since her disappearance ...or at least some...strange apparition resembling her. I always tell them what I'll tell you now: if such a thing were possible, then why would my mother appear to strangers and not to *me*?' He looked distraught now, as though he might burst into tears at any moment.

'Cousin, please, I did not mean to upset you. I—'

'We will say no more about it,' snapped Toby. 'The matter is ended.' He took a deep breath and seemed to get his temper under control. When he spoke again his voice was calmer. 'Well,' he said, 'I'll bid you goodnight, cousin. I've no doubt Mrs Craddock will call you early tomorrow morning.' He picked up the lantern from the table and started to leave, then turned back as though he'd just remembered something. 'Try not to make too much noise on the stairs when you come down,' he said. 'I prefer to lie in of a morning.' He gave William a last, strange look, then let himself out of the room, slamming the door behind him.

William stared after him for a moment, wondering what he had let himself in for. He had thought that there couldn't be a worse place than Mrs Selby's, but at least there he understood everything he encountered. He'd been in this ancient house only a few hours and the place seemed to swarm with mystery.

Why had Seth said such cruel things about William's father? It was almost as though his uncle was baiting him, rubbing salt into his wounds. Worst of all was the realisation that he would not be able to continue with his education, something that meant the world to him. If he hadn't felt so numb, he would have cried.

He realised that, whatever else came or went, he needed to get some sleep. So he untied the blanket from his bundle and flung it over the one on the mattress. He picked up the candle from the table and carried it over to his bed. He sat down and, kicking off his boots, inspected his ruined feet in the candlelight. He longed to wash them, apply some soothing balm, but he had nothing like that and did not much fancy going back down three flights of stairs to ask for some. So he crawled fully clothed under the covers, blew out the candle and closed his eyes.

He was asleep in moments.

CHAPTER FOUR
Awakening

He woke after what seemed like just a few minutes and lay in the darkness, confused, thinking at first that he was back in the workhouse, in the cramped dormitory with the other boys, dreading the tolling of the five o'clock bell, which summoned them to work. But then it all came back to him – his long and arduous trek from Northwich to Wales, his late arrival at Jessop Rise, that strange meal with Uncle Seth and his stepson, Toby. As William's senses came back to him he became aware of pain: a dull throb in his blistered feet from his long walk from Northwich. But it was not that which had woken him.

It was the sound of a woman crying.

He lay on his back, gazing over at the shimmering outline of the dormer window, and listened to that pitiful sound.

It was eerily loud, as though coming from somewhere nearby. Mrs Craddock? She hadn't struck him as the crying kind. He became aware now of how cold it was in the room and he felt, rather than saw, his breath clouding before his face. He was used to being cold, the long winter nights in Northwich had been bad enough, but never like this. The chill seemed to permeate right to his very bones. It occurred to him now that the crying sounded closer – as though it was actually coming from within the room in which he lay.

The realisation galvanised him into full wakefulness. He sat up and peered into the darkness, but could see nothing. Then he remembered the candle and box of matches on the floor beside the mattress, so he reached out a hand and began to pat the bare floorboards, sweeping his arm from side to side in an attempt to locate them, but he must have been trying in the wrong place, because his questing fingers found nothing and now it seemed to him as though the crying was getting even louder, the weeping becoming ever more frantic and inconsolable until it must surely fill the entire house with its sound. He thrust out his hand a second time, and with a suddenness that snatched the breath right out of him, somebody put the box of matches into his hand.

He flinched away with a gasp of terror, pushing himself back against the wall to his right-hand side. He could hardly control his breathing now, and when he tried to speak his voice was little more than a ragged whisper. 'Who... who's there?' he hissed.

There was no reply, but the crying continued.

'Please,' he said, 'who is it?'

Nothing: only the sobbing, which was rising steadily in volume, a symphony of utter misery. The box of matches was still clenched tight in his left fist, so with shaking hands he opened it and clumsily extracted a single match. He struck it hard against the side of the box and it flared, filling the room with a harsh yellow light. And he saw, with a thrill of absolute terror, that the room was completely empty. And yet the crying continued unabated.

'Please,' whimpered William, gazing frantically around. 'Who... who's there? Please, stop crying.'

Quite suddenly, as though obeying his entreaty, the sound stopped. The silence that followed was somehow infinitely worse.

William licked his dry lips. 'Show yourself,' he said, but even as he said it he knew he didn't *want* to see whoever was responsible for waking him. He waited, hardly daring to breathe, but nothing happened. 'What do you want?' he whispered at last.

There was another long silence and then a desperate reply, two words spoken at a volume that shook him to the core.

'Help me!'

William could hardly breathe, such was his terror. 'How...how can I...?'

The flame burned his fingers and he dropped the match with a yelp of pain, plunging the room back into darkness. Panic rippled through him. Now there was a strange, drawn-out hissing noise, as though the woman, whoever she was, was letting out a long breath. William scrabbled with the box and managed to extract another match. As he did so, he thought he was aware of something moving towards him in the darkness, and he was on the point of crying out in terror when his clumsy fingers finally managed to scrape another match against the side of the box.

Once again, light flooded the room.

And once again, there was nobody there. He sat in his bed, staring around in wide-eyed wonder, his whole body trembling beneath the blankets. He was completely alone. Beside the bed stood the candle in its tin holder, though he could have sworn it was exactly where he had been patting the ground just moments ago. He leaned over with the match and lit the wick, giving the room a stronger, more permanent illumination.

He told himself that he must have been dreaming, but if that were the case, how was he to explain the stinging sensation of a recent burn to the tip of his finger and thumb? He sat there looking at his hand and then lifted his head, alarmed, as the door of his room creaked slowly open and fresh light illuminated the figure of a woman standing in the doorway.

William let out a sigh of relief. It was Mrs Craddock, dressed in a white nightgown, the thick shawl around her shoulders, a candle and holder held out in front of her. The look on her face was one of irritation. 'What's going on in yure?' she whispered. 'I heard noises.'

He gazed at her apologetically. 'I...I woke up,' he said. 'I...I thought I heard someone.' He looked hopeful. 'It wasn't you, was it?'

She gave him a disapproving look. 'What are you talking about, boy?'

'I...I thought I heard a woman crying. And then she said...'

Her eyes narrowed suspiciously. 'Said what?' she asked him.

But somehow he couldn't bring himself to tell her what he had heard. It seemed to him that it would sound ridiculous. And in that moment he also knew that she would not believe a single word of it. 'I...I think perhaps I was dreaming,' he said.

She sniffed, scowled, moved closer. 'You need to keep quiet at night,' she told him. 'If you wake Mr Jessop, there will be hell to pay.'

He nodded. 'I'm sorry,' he said.

'We'd *all* be sorry,' she assured him. 'He has a fierce temper when he's roused. You'd do well to remember that.'

'I'll try,' he said.

She seemed to soften a little. 'I appreciate it's not easy for you, coming all the way out yure to this strange place and you so young and everything. It will take some getting used to, that's for sure.'

'Have you...worked here long?' he asked her, glad now to have somebody to talk to.

Her face seemed to light up. 'Oh, for many years. I was yure when it was still Ransome Rise.' She smiled as though recalling happier days. 'The old master was a different sort of man entirely. An officer and a gentleman he was.' Then a sour look took over. 'I've learned since that if you want to get along yure, you have to turn a blind eye to certain things...and you need to know when to keep your trap shut.' She frowned, as though she might have said too much. 'How did you get on with Master Toby?' she asked.

William shook his head. 'Not so very well,' he admitted. 'At first everything was pleasant enough, but then I said something to make him lose his temper and...for a moment there I thought he was going to hit me.'

Mrs Craddock made a tutting sound. 'I won't say I'm surprised. For all that the lad is no blood kin to Mr Jessop, he still has the same kind of temper. He's learned those ways, mind you. He used to be a gentle lad, when the old master was yure. Now he's...changed. He took it bad when his mother disappeared, you see. They were so close, the two of them, such good friends. Some would say she spoiled him rotten, but who can blame a mother for that?' She sighed. 'What did you say that he took such exception to?'

'Well, it...it was...'

'Go on, boy, spit it out.'

'I told him that I'd seen a woman...'

'A woman?"

'Yes, on the way up here. I told him that she was sitting on the rocks up on the cliff path. He seemed to think I was lying.'

Mrs Craddock gave him a scornful look. 'It's lonely out yure,' she said. 'Easy to let your imagination run away with you. Little wonder you're having bad dreams. But be careful what you say to Master Toby. He's had a lot to contend with, what with his mother going missing and everything. And people can be cruel, you know. There's many who have said things to him... about his mother... about what might have happened to her. In a small community like this one, people will gossip, and often it's based on nothing more than idle talk. My advice would be to just smile and nod and do as he tells you. You'll get along better if you do that.'

'I'll... try,' said William.

She turned away and headed back to the door. 'Now, I would suggest that you get some sleep,' she said over her shoulder. 'We've both got an early start in the morning. And mind you don't leave that candle burning all night. The last thing we need in this place is a fire.'

She went out of the room, closing the door behind her, and he heard her creaking footsteps going along the landing to her room. He sighed and shook his head, convinced that she knew a lot more than she was letting on. He lay down again and stared at the guttering light of the candle flame, a few inches from his head. He reminded himself that Mrs

Craddock had warned him to blow it out, but somehow he couldn't bring himself to. So he just lay there staring at it, and the next time he knew anything, the early morning sun was spilling in through the dormer window and Mrs Craddock was at the door, telling him to get up. He looked guiltily at the candle, expecting to see that it had melted clean away. But it was back on the little table and had burned down only an inch or so before somebody had blown it out.

CHAPTER FIVE
THE WELL

William went quietly down the stairs and found his way to the kitchen, where Mrs Craddock stood at a huge cast-iron range, stirring something grey in a saucepan, something that bubbled and hissed. She glanced up as he came in and pointed to a big pine table in the centre of the room.

'Have a seat,' she told him. 'The porridge won't be long.'

He did as he was told. 'Mrs Craddock,' he asked politely, 'did you . . . by any chance blow out my candle last night?'

She gave him an odd look. 'I did not,' she said. 'I seem to remember that I told *you* to do that.'

He was about to say that somebody else must have, when a door on the far side of the kitchen opened and a young girl came in, carrying a wooden bowl heaped with muddy potatoes. She was a scrawny thing, perhaps eleven or twelve years old, William decided, with a thin, pale face and lank red hair that hung to her shoulders. She wore a shapeless grey dress over which was tied a grubby white pinafore. 'Ah, now here's Rhiannon,' said Mrs Craddock. 'Rhiannon, come here and say hullo to William. He's Mr Jessop's nephew and he's going to be living yure.'

The girl turned her large green eyes in William's direction and performed a sort of curtsy. 'Never mind the airs and graces,' Mrs Craddock told her. 'He'll be a worker, the same as you and me.' Rhiannon looked puzzled at this, but she nodded to William, then carried her bowl over to a worktop and started emptying out its contents. 'Rhiannon is our scullery maid,' explained Mrs Craddock helpfully. 'She lives in the village. Walks up yure every morning to work and goes home again at night.'

'Pleased to meet you,' said William. He couldn't think of anything else to add to that.

Mrs Craddock spooned a thin grey slop into a wooden bowl and brought it over to the table. She set it down in front of William and handed him a wooden spoon. He stared doubtfully at the porridge but didn't dare risk passing comment. He wondered if there was anything sweet to go with it, and Mrs Craddock must have read his thoughts, because she indicated an earthenware pot in the middle of the table. 'There's some honey,' she told him. 'Don't go taking too much,' she warned him, as he reached for it. 'Precious stuff, that is, and we'll have no more until the spring.' He nodded and poured just a little of the golden substance into his bowl, then stirred it around. He took a mouthful of the porridge and tried not to grimace. Even with the addition of honey, the overwhelming flavour was of salt.

'That'll stick to your ribs,' observed Mrs Craddock. She went over to stand beside Rhiannon, helping her to sort through the potatoes. 'You'll always need to speak English to William,' she told the girl. 'He doesn't speak God's own language. He has walked all the way from Northwich. That's over eighty miles.'

Rhiannon turned briefly to glance at William. She looked impressed. 'Northwich is in England, is it?' she asked.

William nodded. 'It's in Cheshire,' he said, proud of his knowledge.

Her expression suggested she had no idea what that meant. 'My father went to England once,' she said. 'To Chester. He said it wasn't really all that different to Wales. Only that people spoke odd.'

'Chester is in Cheshire too,' he told her.

'I thought it was in England,' she said, looking confused, so he decided not to pursue the matter any further.

Mrs Craddock smiled and busied herself at the stove. 'Me, I've never been further than Porthmadog,' she said, sounding almost proud of the fact. 'My old mother always used to say, if you have to travel to something, it probably isn't worth the effort.'

William frowned. He didn't think he'd get on at all well with Mrs Craddock's mother. He kept spooning the porridge into his mouth, but hungry as he was, it took considerable effort to swallow it.

'Rhiannon's father works at the slate quarry,' said Mrs Craddock. 'He's a foreman there. It was quite an honour for him when the master invited her to come and work at Jessop Rise.'

Rhiannon gave a wan smile at this, as though she didn't really think it *was* that much of an honour but was too polite to say.

William managed to swallow the last spoonful of porridge and pushed his bowl aside. Mrs Craddock indicated a black jacket that was draped over the back of a chair beside him. 'That's for you,' she said. 'Try it on.'

'But...I already have a jacket,' said William.

'That's a hall boy's coat,' said Mrs Craddock patiently. 'It's from the days when they had proper servants yure.'

William found this remark puzzling. 'Don't they any more?' he asked.

'No, they do not,' said Mrs Craddock sourly. 'There's me, there's Rhiannon and now there's you, and that's about the extent of it.'

'There's *Idris*,' Rhiannon reminded her.

'Oh yes, and Idris. I always forget about him.'

'Who is Idris?' asked William, intrigued.

'Just the stableboy. You needn't concern yourself with *him*. He never sets foot in the house. He tends to the horses. He's got more in common with them than he has with people.' She waved a hand as if dismissing the subject. 'In Mr Ransome's day, of course, we had ten servants in this house and everything ran smooth as freshly ironed cotton. Now we're expected to do the work of ten people for a tenth of the pay.' She shook her head in a long-suffering way. 'Mr Jessop doesn't believe in having lots of staff,' she explained. 'He...likes to keep a tight grip on the purse strings.' She looked as though she might be about to say more on the subject, but she must have thought better of it. She shook her head. 'Well, come along, boy. Don't just sit there! Try the jacket on.'

He got up from his seat, removed his own coat and

slipped on the black one. It was apparent in an instant that it was much too big for him, the sleeves hanging down past his fingers, the hem almost to his knees. Mrs Craddock frowned. 'Yes, well, that's only to be expected, I suppose. That belonged, if I remember correctly, to Tom Bevan, who was a good deal stouter than you and head and shoulders higher. Turn the sleeves back for now and I'll have a go at it with a needle and thread tonight.'

William did as she suggested, but he didn't really see why it was necessary for him to wear a special jacket. He glanced sternly at Rhiannon, who, he sensed, was stifling a laugh.

'Right, that will have to do for now,' said Mrs Craddock. 'You can go to the well with Rhiannon and bring back a couple of buckets of water. She'll show you where it is.' She turned her attention back to the potatoes. Rhiannon wiped her muddy hands on her pinafore and gestured for William to follow her. She led him through to a small adjoining room, where there were large stone sinks and work surfaces piled high with saucepans of all shapes and sizes. In one corner there was a stone hearth containing a large 'copper', a cast-iron boiler, which William supposed was for washing clothes and bedding. There was an opening beneath it where a log fire could be kindled, and a large pile of cut logs was stacked beside it. Rhiannon located a couple of wooden buckets with rope handles and tight-fitting lids. She handed one of them to William. 'The well is at the back of the house,' she explained. 'Up at the top of the garden.'

William was impressed. In Northwich, Nora, the maid, had had to fetch their water from the town pump, which often involved much time spent waiting in line.

Rhiannon opened a door at the back of the scullery and stepped out into the garden. The sun was just coming up over the horizon, the spreading light dappling the trees and shrubs. William stood for a moment, gazing around in surprise. The garden was enormous. To his left a high stone wall formed one of its boundaries, but to his right the land stretched as far as he could see. It had evidently once been a delightful place, but was now in urgent need of some restoration. The paths were dotted with ugly clumps of moss, the flowerbeds overgrown to the point where the various blooms were fighting the weeds for space. A vast stretch of lawn had grown straggly and was infested with dandelions and wild daisies. Over to his right William could see what looked like stables, and he noticed a pale-faced figure at a high window. 'There's somebody watching us,' he said.

Rhiannon glanced up. 'Oh, that's just Idris,' she said. 'Ignore him.'

William frowned. 'What did Mrs Craddock mean when she said that he never sets foot in the house?'

An odd look crossed her face. 'Exactly that. He's not one for houses, Idris. He prefers the open air.' She smiled mysteriously. 'Don't worry – I'm sure you'll meet him soon enough.'

'This garden is...huge!' said William. 'I've never seen one like it before.'

She nodded. 'Well, you get used to it after a while, but the first time I set eyes on it, I was just like you.' She mimicked his open-mouthed expression. 'It must have been lovely back in the day, when they had proper gardeners here. But Mr Jessop let them all go.'

'He dismissed them?' asked William, and Rhiannon nodded.

'Them and just about everybody else that worked on the estate,' she said.

'The estate?'

'Oh yes. Mr Jessop owns hundreds of acres of land beyond here, but he got rid of everyone. The gamekeeper, the handyman...even a couple of tenant farmers and their families.' She set off down a weed-strewn path and William followed her.

'Why? Did they do something wrong?'

Rhiannon shook her head and glanced warily around before replying. She seemed suddenly uncomfortable. 'You're Mr Jessop's nephew, so . . . I expect you are close friends with him and Master Toby? I wouldn't want to say anything that might get me into trouble.'

'Oh, don't worry about that,' said William. 'To tell you the truth, I hardly heard tell of them before last night.'

'Really? That's odd.'

'Well, my father went his own way years ago. I think he had fallen out with his father, and he never said much about Uncle Seth.'

'I thought it was odd that Mr Jessop has you working here. His own flesh and blood and everything.'

'He . . . seems a strange man. I . . . well, to be honest, I didn't warm to him. He seemed to take too much pleasure in my misfortune.' He frowned. 'You were telling me about the gardeners?' he prompted her.

Rhiannon seemed reassured. 'Oh yes, three of them there were. Mrs Craddock told me that they'd done nothing wrong. They worked around the clock to keep the grounds looking nice. But one day, soon after Mistress Audrina disappeared, Mr Jessop just marched up to them and gave them their notice. Said they were costing him too much. The truth is, he's a . . . well, there's no other word for it that I can think of. He's a right old miser. Don't you be telling anybody I said that, mind!'

'I won't,' William assured her.

'That man wouldn't spend a farthing unless it was a matter of life or death. And even then, he'd think long and hard on it.'

William frowned. 'Mrs Craddock did say that he keeps a tight hold on the purse strings.'

'Hah! That's not the half of it. He's probably the richest man in Wales, yet you'd never guess it from the state of this place.' She gestured around at the dilapidated garden. 'Look at it! You'd think it belonged to a pauper. But within days of Mistress Audrina going missing, he started ridding himself of every member of staff one by one, all except for Mrs Craddock.'

'Were you here then?' William asked her.

'Oh no, I started three months ago, and then only because Mrs Craddock begged Mr Jessop for some help around the place.' She shook her head. 'But mark you, even that had to be done on *his* terms.'

'What do you mean?' asked William.

'Mr Jessop approached my father and offered him the chance to send me to work here, but at half the normal wage! Of course my father was too afraid for his own job at the quarry to say no. So here I am.' She gave William a shrewd look. 'What are they paying *you*?' she asked him.

William stiffened. 'Nobody has even mentioned money,' he snapped. 'I don't suppose they'll offer me a wage. I was in a workhouse before this so ... I suppose he thinks I should be grateful I have a roof over my head.'

Rhiannon smiled grimly. 'Yes, now why does this not surprise me? You take my advice, William, mention money at your first opportunity, because Mr Jessop *never* will.' She seemed to register what he'd just said. 'A workhouse?' she murmured. 'What happened to your parents?'

William shook his head. 'My mother died years ago,' he said, 'when I was little. And my father was killed in a factory accident in May.'

'Oh dear,' said Rhiannon. 'I'm sorry for your loss.'

They walked on along the path in silence for a few moments. William was pondering the strangeness of his situation. Was that why Uncle Seth had summoned him here, he wondered, simply because he knew that he could get his nephew to work for free? Could anybody be *that* miserly?

'Mrs Craddock said that you and Master Toby had a disagreement,' said Rhiannon, breaking into his thoughts.

'Yes,' he said. 'He was very cross. I thought he was going to hit me.'

'And why would he do that to his own cousin?'

William wasn't sure whether to tell her the real reason, but after quick consideration he couldn't think of anything else to say. 'It's just that I told him that I had seen a woman on the way here.'

'A woman?'

'Yes. Toby seemed to think that I was lying.'

Rhiannon turned for a moment and gave him a sly look. 'When was this?' she asked.

'Late last night. I was coming across the clifftop and—'

'A woman in a cloak?' interrupted Rhiannon.

'Yes!' William quickened his pace to catch up with her, the empty wooden bucket bashing against his shins as he did so. 'Have you seen her too?'

Rhiannon shook her head. 'No, never, thank goodness.

But plenty of others have. She's all too familiar in these parts. The *Gwrach*.'

For a moment William thought that she was clearing her throat in order to spit, but then he realised that the sound she'd made was an actual word. 'The . . . *what*?' he asked.

'The *Gwrach y Rhibyn*. It means . . . the witch or . . . what's the English name for her? Oh yes – the Hag of the Mist. She comes when somebody is going to die.'

'Oh, like the Banshee?' said William.

'What's that?"

'There was an old Irish woman who lived near us in Northwich. She was always telling me stories of when she was little and there was this thing that came howling around people's houses late at night, just before somebody died. The Banshee was what *she* called it.'

Rhiannon shrugged. 'I never heard of that one. But there's plenty of people in these parts who have seen the *Gwrach y Rhibyn*, you mark my words. Including my own father!'

'Really?'

'Oh yes. He told me once that he was walking over the clifftops and he wanted to take the short cut back to the village, so he had to take the track that goes past the stones . . .'

'The what?'

'It's just a circle of standing stones. Very old it is, from the times before they had proper churches, you know?'

'Oh, I think I saw them too. Far off in the distance. They are up on top of a hill, are they not?'

She nodded. 'They belonged to the druids. You'll have heard of them, I suppose? The pagan priests?'

He hadn't, but he let her continue.

'Well, my father was walking along the track and a mist came down all sudden like, as thick as anything, and then he heard this loud shriek, like some kind of bird calling... and all of a sudden there she was, standing in the middle of the circle on the old altar, just watching him go by. A hideous old hag she was, with blood caked all around her mouth.' Rhiannon made an ugly face to try to convey the woman's haggard features. 'Wailing and carrying on something terrible! Well, my father didn't hang around, I can tell you!'

'I don't expect he did!' said William, trying not to smile.

'No, he ran. And the very next day, what do you think happened?'

'I don't know,' admitted William.

'Up at the slate quarry, there were two men killed by falling rocks.' She nodded her head as if she had just given him absolute proof of the creature's existence. 'There now!' She nodded her head a final time as if to emphasise the point. 'Did you...did you see the woman's face?'

William shook his head. 'She was wearing a hood. It was in shadow.'

'Be thankful for that! They say she's hideous. She has black teeth too, you know...and horrible staring eyes. My father said they were the worst eyes he's ever looked into. He said it was like looking into the fires of hell. Was it foggy late last night?'

'Er...no...not at all.'

'That's strange. She usually brings down a mist with her.'

'Well, not last night.'

'And did she have wings?' The question was asked in all seriousness.

'Uh...I...don't think so.'

'Could have been under her cloak, I suppose. Horrible, leathery things they are. So she can flap up to bedroom windows and suck the blood of babies. They say that when the moon is full...'

She broke off as William began to chuckle. He couldn't

help himself. His father had brought him up to scorn such tales. And he remembered what Toby had said about the locals and their superstitious stories. 'I'm sorry,' he said. 'It's all . . . a bit—'

'Suit yourself,' snapped Rhiannon, and hurried on along the path.

'No, please don't be angry,' he pleaded, following her. 'It's only . . . well, don't you think it's a bit fanciful? I'm sure this was just an ordinary woman.'

'Oh yes, because there must be hundreds of perfectly normal ladies who like to sit out on the cliffs in the middle of the night.'

'Well, I suppose it *was* a bit strange,' admitted William. 'Now I think on it.'

'More than strange,' Rhiannon assured him. 'It's the devil's work. What was she doing, this woman?'

'Well, she was . . .'

'Yes?'

'She was just . . . watching the house.'

'*This* house?' Rhiannon scowled and made the sign of the cross. 'I do not like the sound of that at all.' She seemed to think for a moment. 'When you saw her . . . did she . . . did she make a noise? Crying or wailing?'

'No, she . . . actually she bid me good evening.' He didn't mention how the sound of the woman's deep voice had chilled his blood.

Rhiannon grimaced. 'Usually she's sobbing,' she said – and William was reminded of the sounds that had woken him in the night.

'I . . . thought I heard a woman crying last night though,' he said. 'It woke me up.'

Rhiannon gave him a wary look. 'That's it then,' she said woefully. 'Somebody at the Rise will be next. You mark my words.'

They were finally approaching a stone well at the top end of the garden. William could see that it had once had a slate roof, but much of that had collapsed, leaving it mostly open to the sky. There was a circular stone parapet jutting up chest-high from the ground with a simple wooden hoist fixed across it. A round metal lid covered the opening. Rhiannon put down her bucket, lifted the lid with two hands and set it on the ground. Then she and William leaned over the parapet and peered down into the well. Some twenty feet below them a pool of clear water shimmered invitingly, and they could see their own reflections silhouetted against a circle of blue sky.

'Hullo!' shouted Rhiannon, and her voice echoed back to her. 'The best-tasting water in the county,' she assured William. 'It's fed by a stream deep underground. I wish it was a bit closer to the house though.' There was a wooden bucket on a rope attached to the hoist. Rhiannon lifted it and let it fall into the well. The handle spun as the weighted bucket plummeted to the water. It sank quickly below the surface and then Rhiannon and William cranked the handle to lift the bucket back to the top of the shaft. In this way they were able to fill their own buckets, and once this was done Rhiannon hefted hers by its rope handle and pointed to the metal well cover. 'Put that back on, will you?' she said.

William picked up the lid and stepped back to the parapet. He glanced down into the water and there was his own reflection, staring back up at him. He opened his mouth to shout something, but his voice trailed off as he became aware of a second reflection, standing just behind him and peering over his shoulder, a tall hooded silhouette. William spun around with a gasp of surprise, only to find that he was alone. Rhiannon had already started back along the path to the house and was some distance away, struggling to carry her load. William turned back and stared down, once again, into the well. Only his own reflection gazed back at him.

My imagination getting the better of me, he told himself. Rhiannon's wild talk of the *Gwrach* must have stirred him up. He slid the metal cover back into position with a dull clunk.

'Come along, slowcoach!' Rhiannon mocked.

He went to his bucket and hefted it by the rope handle, realising as he followed her along the path, back to the house, that Rhiannon must be a lot stronger than her scrawny figure suggested.

CHAPTER SIX
MASTER TOBY'S BREAKFAST

Back in the kitchen they found Mrs Craddock frying eggs, sausages and rashers of bacon in a large black pan. The intense smell of cooking meat made William's stomach lurch. His meagre breakfast had done little to satisfy his hunger.

'You were a long time fetching that water,' said Mrs Craddock. 'I hope that's not an example of your usual speed.'

William didn't know what to say to that. He followed Rhiannon into the scullery and they set down their full buckets before returning to the kitchen. 'Rhiannon, you can make a start on resetting the fire in the dining room,' said Mrs Craddock, and the girl headed dutifully away. 'William, you can take Master Toby's breakfast up to him.'

William watched enviously as she transferred the cooked breakfast onto a plate and that onto a tray together with cutlery, bread, a cup and saucer, a jug of milk, a silver pot of tea and a linen napkin. 'His bedroom is on the first floor,' she told William. 'It's the first door as you step onto the landing. Well, hurry along, boy, or the food will be cold!'

William lifted the tray and set off, trying not to look at the food as he walked, because he knew he'd be tempted to pick up one of those rashers of crispy bacon and cram it into his mouth. A few moments later he was tapping on Toby's door, the tray held precariously in one hand.

'Go away,' said a voice from within. William scowled and tried not to think about the meagre breakfast he'd just eaten.

'Toby, it's me. William. I've brought your breakfast.'

There was a long groan and then Toby said, 'Oh very well, I suppose you'd better come in.'

William opened the door and stepped inside. He stood for a moment, staring into the gloom. The heavy drapes were closed, allowing barely any light into the room, which appeared to be large and expensively furnished, though not much of the furniture was actually visible, due to the fact that it was covered in piles of discarded clothing, heaps of footwear and various bits and pieces of equipment that didn't even seem to belong in a bedroom. Peering around, William identified what looked like a leather saddle, a couple of muskets, a telescope, various books, piles of papers and a lot more besides. A four-poster bed stood on the far side of the room and lying in it, propped up on a mound of pillows, was Toby. He was wearing a white nightshirt, and looked pretty indignant at being roused from his sleep.

'What time is it?' he protested.

'Around eight o'clock, I think,' offered William.

Toby scowled. 'Eight?' he muttered. 'What's got into the old battle-axe?' William supposed he was referring to Mrs Craddock. 'She *knows* I don't like to be woken until ten.'

William could only shrug. 'She told me to bring your breakfast up,' he said. 'It's getting cold,' he added.

'Oh, bring it over,' said Toby wearily, as though being required to eat was a terrible imposition. He gestured to a bedside table. 'Set it there a moment while you get those curtains open. I'd like to be able to see what I'm eating.'

William moved obediently across to the bed, picking his way through the various heaps of debris that littered the floorboards. He set down the tray and, moving to the drapes, he pulled them back, allowing the bright morning sunshine to spill into the room. Now William could see down into the back garden where he had just been. Up at the far end of it, the well looked reassuringly deserted.

'Well, come along,' Toby urged him. 'I'll be dead of hunger by the time you stir yourself into action.' William turned back and handed the tray to Toby, though he couldn't help feeling that the boy was close enough to have reached it for himself. Toby took the tray grudgingly and scowled at its contents as though he'd been presented with a tray of dog mess. 'The same every morning,' he complained. 'She never varies.' He glanced at William. 'Tea?' he said.

'No, thank you,' said William.

Toby glared at him. 'I'm not offering you some, you clod,' he snapped. 'I'm telling you to pour it!'

'Oh ... sorry.'

'You haven't got much idea about being a valet, have you?'

'Well, I've never been one before.' William stepped closer and tried to figure out what to do. He located a silver strainer and placed that over the cup, then poured tea into it from the pot. Toby, meanwhile, picked a fat sausage from his plate and took a huge bite. Grease trickled down his chin and he wiped it away with the sleeve of his nightshirt. William tried hard not to notice. 'Will you have milk?' he asked.

'Of course,' said Toby, through a mouthful of meat. 'That's how all young gentlemen take their tea these days.' He studied William thoughtfully. 'Have you had *your* breakfast yet?' he asked.

William nodded. 'Yes, thank you,' he said.

'Let me guess,' murmured Toby, crunching a mouthful of bacon now. 'Mrs Craddock's famous porridge? Hideous stuff. One doesn't know whether to eat it or to use it as mortar to repoint the house.'

'It was...a little salty,' admitted William.

'She offered me some of that stuff once,' said Toby. '"It will make a change," she said.' He smiled grimly. 'I threw the bowl at the wall and told her never to make that mistake again.' He studied William thoughtfully for a moment. 'Look,' he said, 'I'm sorry about last night. I do feel dashed bad about it, but it was your own fault really. You shouldn't have lied to me. That always gets my goat.'

William thought about protesting that he hadn't been lying, but decided that might not be his wisest move. 'I was speaking to Rhiannon,' he said. 'She told me about some strange witch that's supposed to haunt this area.'

Toby rolled his eyes. 'There you are, you see. *That's* what I was talking about. If you listen to the locals, you'll hear nothing else: there's a ghost that haunts one thing and a witch that guards another... It's as though they're still living in the Middle Ages! But talk to them about science and they look at you as though you're speaking a different language. You don't believe in such nonsense, do you, cousin?'

'Er...no. No, of course not.' There was a long silence. 'Well,' said William. 'I'd... better get back down to the kitchen.' He started to move away.

'No, wait a minute. What's the big hurry?' Toby glanced at him slyly. 'I expect you could help me to eat the rest of this food, couldn't you?'

William tried not to stare at the plate. 'Oh, that's... all right,' he said, but even to his own ears his voice lacked conviction, and the grumbling sound in his stomach betrayed him audibly.

'Don't be ridiculous,' insisted Toby. 'Go on, take a sausage.'

Now William raised his eyes to the plate. 'I shouldn't really,' he said. 'What if Mrs Craddock finds out?'

'Who's going to tell her? Certainly not me.' Toby smiled as though savouring the feeling of power this gave him. 'Go on, cousin. Help yourself. Think of it as an apology for last night.'

William couldn't fight it any longer. He reached out a hand and snatched up one of the sausages, then tore into it, taking huge mouthfuls and chewing frantically.

'Slow down,' Toby advised him. 'You'll give yourself indigestion.' He smiled. 'I expect you could eat some bread with that?'

This time William reacted immediately, snatching up a slice of bread, folding it around what was left of the sausage and devouring the two together.

'You see,' said Toby, 'I'm not so bad really. We'll get along famously, you and I, just as long as you behave yourself.' He lifted a rasher of bacon to his own mouth and chewed thoughtfully as he looked around his room. 'So...valet. I have a little job for you,' he said.

'Do you?' William managed to drag his gaze from what was left on Toby's plate. 'What's that then?'

'This room. It's in a frightful state, don't you think?'

William looked around. 'It *is* a bit of a mess,' he admitted.

'It would be really helpful if you'd clean it up for me.'

'Oh, er... very well. When would you like me to...?'

'You may as well start now,' said Toby. He lifted his cup of tea and slurped at it. 'The clothes can go in the wardrobe over there...' He waved his free hand. 'The books will go on the writing desk. And so on...If you're not sure about something, just ask me.'

'I think Mrs Craddock was expecting me back in the kitchen,' said William.

'*I'll* take care of Mrs Craddock,' said Toby. 'That woman needs to learn her place. After all, she's only a *servant*. And you're supposed to be *my* valet, aren't you? What's the point of sharing you with her?' William couldn't help thinking how changeable Toby could be, pleasant one moment, vindictive the next. He had spoken about Mrs Craddock as though working people were of no consequence at all.

William set about clearing the room, a task which, he could see, was going to take some time. He began by gathering up the various jackets, waistcoats and breeches that lay around the room. When he opened the huge wardrobe he found plenty of shelves in there to stack them on. He didn't really see why Toby couldn't clear up after himself. William's father had always insisted that he keep his little room in Northwich tidy at all times. But he didn't want to anger Toby, so he set about the task without complaint. At least his stomach had quietened down a bit after the extra helping of food. As he worked, Toby kept up a constant stream of conversation from his bed.

'Don't hang that up,' he said pointing to a jacket William had been about to fold. 'I'll wear that today. You can put it at the foot of the bed. Oh, and those trousers too. Yes, the green velvet ones. Put them there.' He took another slurp of tea. 'So, tell me, William, what was your father like?'

'My father?' William struggled to the wardrobe with several garments draped across his shoulders. 'Oh, he was...a good man. A hard worker.'

'And he wanted you to follow in his footsteps, I suppose. To go into the...what was it? The cotton industry?'

William shook his head. 'Oh no. He always said he wanted something better for me. That's why he sent me to school.'

'School!' Toby blew air out from between pursed lips. 'I used to have tutors here when my mother...before she...' He waved a hand. 'Oh yes, I was quite the scholar. Mathematics...science...even Latin! But my stepfather dispensed with the tutors as soon as Mother was no longer around.'

William folded each garment as neatly as he could and stacked them onto the shelves, trying to group similar items together. 'Why do you suppose he did that?' he asked.

'Didn't you hear him last night? Seth doesn't believe in education. He's a self-made man.'

William frowned. 'Not really,' he said. 'Didn't he say that he inherited the quarry from my grandfather?'

'Well, that's true, enough, I suppose. But the old man surely *was* self-made; he had no education to speak of, just a working knowledge of the quarrying business. He lived here for a year or so in his last days, so I got to know him a bit.'

'What was he like?'

'He was...a simple soul,' said Toby. 'But he had a good head for business. When he started, that quarry was little more than a scrape in the earth. He worked hard and made it a success, but Seth is the one that turned it into what it is now...the most profitable quarry in Wales.' Toby laughed. 'You know, Seth is actually proud of his lack of schooling? He always maintains that most teachers are idiots and not to be trusted.' Toby sniggered. 'My Latin tutor, Mr Carswell, tried to argue that Seth was making a big mistake by dispensing with his services. Seth boxed his ears and sent him packing! What do you think of that?'

William shrugged. What he actually thought was that Toby had been denied a golden opportunity to further his education. But he could hardly say that. 'I'm not sure *what* to think about it,' he said. He turned to look at Toby. 'What do *you* think? Did you enjoy your lessons?'

'Not particularly. I much prefer idling. But of course I suppose I *will* have to do a bit of work when I finally come into my inheritance.' He thought for a moment. 'I believe my real father would have liked me to go into the military, just as he did, but I cannot imagine what that would be like, marching about and obeying orders . . . sticking your head up above a parapet and inviting some cove to take a potshot at it. It sounds most tiresome.' He studied William for a moment. 'What were you hoping to do?'

'What do you mean?'

'Well, I cannot believe it was your deepest wish to be my lackey.'

'Oh no, of course not! I . . . well, I . . . had a flair for science. I had hoped that one day, I might . . .'

'Might what?'

'Be a . . . doctor?'

Toby laughed at this. 'Another profession that my stepfather despises!' he observed. 'He always maintains that not one of them is worth the money he's paid. He says they are all quacks.'

'He seems a hard man, Uncle Seth.'

'Oh, you do not know the half of it! Why, I've seen him...' He broke off, shaking his head as if reluctant to continue.

'What have you seen?' William prompted him, as he slid another garment into the wardrobe.

'We were in the village once and there was a beggar standing beside the doorway of a shop where we needed to go in. An old man, on crutches, he was, very thin and grey-haired. He held out a tin cup to Seth and asked for coins. My stepfather cursed him and kicked one of his crutches away, sent him sprawling in to the road. Told him that he should be ashamed of himself begging for money, that he should go out and find work. But this poor old fellow, he was barely strong enough to keep himself upright. Seth just stepped over him and went about his business. And once we were inside, he said to me...'

'Yes?'

'He told me to mark what he had done and to always keep it in mind. "Charity begins at home," he said. And he told me to be aware that the world lies ever in wait for the wallets of soft-hearted fools.'

William was shocked by the story. 'I wonder what made

him so stern,' he murmured.

'I imagine it was the way he was raised. You know the old saying: "Spare the rod and spoil the child." I think your grandfather was a hard taskmaster. For all that my father was a soldier, he never raised a hand to me in anger.'

But my father wasn't like that, thought William, and he was raised by the same hands as Seth. He thought about mentioning this, but decided against it. He remembered Mrs Craddock's advice to agree with whatever Toby said. He placed the last pair of breeches on a shelf and then turned to look at the rest of the room. He pointed at the leather saddle. 'What would you have me do with that?' he asked.

'It needs to go back to the stables,' said Toby. 'Seth wanted me to oil it. I told him that was a servant's job, but he said it would do me good to get my hands dirty for a change. He thinks just because *he* came up from nothing, the rest of us should experience it once in a while. Anyway, I brought it up here to do it, where it was warmer. And I don't much care for that idiot of a stableboy.'

'Oh, Idris? I've not met him yet.'

'Be thankful for small mercies,' said Toby uncharitably. 'He's a halfwit.'

William wasn't sure what to say to that. 'You...ride then?' he asked.

Toby scowled. 'Not as well as I should,' he admitted. 'My father, of course, was keen for me to learn from an early age, but after he was gone, there was nobody to encourage me. Oh, Seth can ride well enough, but he takes no great pleasure in it. And when he does go out on horseback he prefers his own company. He says it is the only time he can think about business matters. What about you? Can you ride?'

William laughed. 'There wasn't much call for horsemanship in Northwich,' he admitted. 'We had a wagon and an old nag...'

At that moment the door of the room opened, revealing the scowling features of Mrs Craddock. The timing of her entrance was unfortunate. Toby laughed out loud and William had to work very hard not to follow his example. Mrs Craddock, however, clearly failed to see anything amusing in the situation.

'William, you've been up yure for ages!' she complained. 'I've a whole list of jobs waiting for you downstairs.'

'Yes, Mrs Craddock. Sorry.' William moved to obey her, but froze in his tracks when Toby's voice spoke up with cool authority.

'Just a moment, William.' William turned back to look at the bed and saw that Toby was appraising Mrs Craddock with evident rebellion in his eyes. 'Mrs Craddock, William is carrying out a task that *I* have set him.'

'That's all well and good, Master Toby, but—'

'It seems to me that the boy was appointed to be *my* assistant, not yours. Perhaps my stepfather didn't make it clear that his main duties lie with me.'

'Well, now, he did say something to that effect, but—'

'But what? It would seem that you are rather overstepping your authority. You have Rhiannon to assist you, do you not?'

Mrs Craddock's pale features had turned a dark shade of red. 'I only wanted him to—'

'Perhaps I should summon my stepfather and ask him to clarify the situation,' suggested Toby. 'I'm sure he'd be happy to oblige.'

For a moment the two of them exchanged glares, but it was Mrs Craddock who weakened first. She bowed her head. 'There's no need for that, Master Toby,' she mumbled. 'Perhaps when William has finished yure, you might send him down to help me with one or two chores?'

Toby smiled coldly. 'Perhaps,' he said. 'I'll think about it.'

'Thank you, Master Toby.' She went to close the door, but he lifted a hand to stop her. 'Oh, before you go, Mrs Craddock –' he nodded to the tray on his lap, the empty plate and cup – 'perhaps you'd be kind enough to take this away?'

There was a long silence. Defiance flared in her eyes and for a moment William thought she was going to slam the door and storm off, but she must have thought better of it, because after a brief hesitation she came into the room, walked over to the bed and obediently took the tray from him.

'I hope breakfast was to your taste,' she said quietly.

'Not bad at all,' he told her. 'The eggs . . .'

'Yes, Master Toby?'

'They weren't quite how I like them. A little too runny. But otherwise, perfectly acceptable.'

'Yes, sir. Thank you, sir.' She turned away and went out of the room, but not before she had thrown a wounded sidelong look at William. The door closed behind her and her heavy footsteps moved away along the landing and then down the stairs.

Toby smirked. 'And that,' he told William, 'is how one deals with troublesome servants.'

William assumed he was supposed to laugh at this remark, but he was painfully aware that he himself was now a servant and that Toby wasn't always in such a friendly mood. So he just nodded and went on with the job of tidying the room, while Toby watched from his bed.

CHAPTER SEVEN
THE STABLEBOY

When William had finally got the room cleaned up to Toby's satisfaction, and helped him to dress himself, he picked up the leather saddle and carried it downstairs, leaving Toby to his own devices. He found Mrs Craddock and Rhiannon down in the kitchen, preparing food. This seemed to be pretty much a full-time occupation for them. Mrs Craddock watched him warily as he approached, carrying the heavy saddle in his arms.

'What are you doing with that thing?' she asked sourly. She seemed to be in a crotchety mood after her exchange of words with Toby.

'Please, Mrs Craddock, Master Toby told me to take it out to the stable,' said William.

'Did he now? That boy's getting a little too big for his boots, if you ask me.' She sighed, glanced at Rhiannon. 'You'd better go with him this time,' she said. 'Idris seems to listen to you. But don't be dawdling, girl – we've a lot to do before dinnertime.'

Rhiannon nodded. She set down the turnip she'd been peeling and beckoned to William to follow her. She led him out through the scullery, which was now warm and smoky, a wood fire blazing under the boiler. Steam billowed from the mouth of it. They went out of the back door into the garden. The sun was directly overhead now, a lovely October day.

'Why do you need to come with me?' William asked her. 'I know where the stable is; you showed me before.'

Rhiannon shook her head. 'Idris can be funny with strangers,' she said.

'What do you mean, "funny"?'

'You'll see,' she assured him. They strolled along the path to the place where it branched off towards the stable, William's arms aching now beneath the weight of the saddle. They walked across the grass in silence. The door was wide open, so Rhiannon stepped inside. 'Yoo-hoo!' she called. 'Idris?'

There seemed to be nobody there. William stood for a moment, looking around. It was a big, roomy place built of rough timber. There were four wooden stalls and he could see the heads of a row of horses gazing placidly out of them.

At the top of the stable there was a large black carriage, of the kind that people usually called a 'growler'. About halfway along the building, a rickety ladder led up to a hayloft. William was struck by how tidy the place was, a far cry from the mess up at the house. Barrels were stacked neatly in a corner and bales of hay arranged one on top of the other in orderly ranks. It was evident that somebody was taking good care of this place. William carried the saddle over to one of the empty stalls and, with a sigh of relief, draped it over the side. He flexed his arms. 'There doesn't seem to be anyone about,' he said.

'Oh, he's here,' said Rhiannon. 'He's shy of strangers, that's all.' She walked over to the foot of the ladder and gazed up into the loft. 'Idris?' she called. 'I know you're up there. Won't you come down and say hullo?'

There was a long silence.

'Oh, come on, Idris, stop playing around!' persisted Rhiannon. 'We've only got a few moments.'

Again, silence. William was just on the point of saying that perhaps they'd better get back to the house, when a head finally popped into view at the top of the ladder. William registered a dirty face, topped by a tousled heap of hair that stuck up in all directions.

'*There* you are!' said Rhiannon. 'Idris, I've brought somebody to meet you. Come down from there, please.'

The dark eyes in the stubbly face studied William with open suspicion. Then an arm lifted and pointed an equally grubby index finger in his direction. Idris asked something in Welsh.

'No, Idris, we're talking English today,' Rhiannon corrected him.

'Ah yes!' Idris pointed again. 'Who's that?' he croaked. 'Who's that boy?'

'This is William,' said Rhiannon calmly. 'He's working at the house now. And he only speaks English.'

'Will'yam?' muttered Idris, as though unfamiliar with the name. 'His name is Will'yam? Idris does not know this name!' Now the arm moved sideways to point to the saddle that William had just set down. 'Saddle don't go there!'

'Oh...I'm sorry.' William turned back towards it. 'Where would you like me to...?' He broke off in surprise as, with a sudden wild lunge, Idris threw himself out of the hayloft and hurtled down to land between William and the stall, performing an ungainly forward roll in the straw. He crouched for a moment, his head twisting this way and that, looking like some kind of wild beast that was protecting his territory. Now William could see him more clearly and judged him to be in his mid-twenties. He was a thin, angular fellow, dressed in a ragged grey shirt that had probably once been white and a pair of torn, tattered breeches. He wore no shoes, William noticed, and his feet were black with dirt. He bared his jagged teeth and made an alarming hissing sound, which prompted William to take an involuntary step back. The man sounded like a feral cat.

'Idris!' scolded Rhiannon. 'Be nice. William is a friend.' She paused to pat William on the head as though he was a pet dog. 'See? Friend,' she repeated. 'William friends with Rhiannon.'

'Friend,' repeated Idris, nodding. 'Will'yam is friend.' He sprang suddenly upright and, hurrying over to the saddle, he lifted it up and carried it to the back of the stable, where William could now see a couple of others arranged on wooden frames. Idris carefully draped the saddle over an empty frame and stroked the glossy leather with his fingertips. 'Nice and clean now,' he said approvingly. 'Mr Jessop made Toby clean his saddle. Idris offered to do it, but Mr Jessop was angry with Toby.' He switched suddenly to a very accurate impersonation of Seth's voice. 'No, Toby, it's your saddle, you clean it! It'll do you good to get your hands dirty for a change!' Idris grinned, then turned back to look at William. 'Saddles always go here,' he said. 'You put them back wrong, Mr Jessop brings out his riding crop.' He made the action of lifting his arm up and down, as though beating an invisible person, making a swishing noise by blowing air out from between his pursed lips. 'You won't like the riding crop,' he murmured. 'Idris don't like the riding crop.'

'I'll...try to remember that,' said William nervously.

'Good!' Now Idris hurried forward and extended a hand to put his index finger against William's lips. 'Your voice sounds...soft,' he observed. 'You are...from Enger-land, yes?'

'Yes,' said William. 'From Northwich. Do you know it?'

Idris shook his head. 'Idris don't know North-widge. But he does know Enger-land.'

'You have been there?' ventured William.

Idris laughed, a short, loud bark of a laugh. 'Oh no! Idris *knows* Enger-land, but never goes there! Idris knows Miss Audrina! *She* is from Enger-land. She is a fine English lady.' He looked suddenly distraught. 'But she's gone now.' He poked William in the chest. 'You know where she's gone?'

'Er...no. No, I'm afraid not.'

'She gone to Enger-land?'

'Perhaps. I . . . I've no idea.'

Idris sighed. He looked perturbed. Now he turned his attention to Rhiannon. 'Miss Rhiannon knows?'

Rhiannon shook her head. 'Nobody knows, Idris. I've told you before. She just went away one night. Gone.'

'She'll come back soon?'

'I don't think so.'

Idris sighed. He looked downcast. Just then, one of the horses in the stall, a haughty-looking black creature, snorted loudly. Idris twisted his head and looked in that direction. 'No, Sabre,' he said. 'No, they say she's gone.'

The horse blew more air through its nostrils, and Idris moved quickly towards the creature and placed his own nose against that of the horse. The two of them snorted at each other for a few moments and William would have felt a powerful desire to laugh at their antics, except that it really did look as though they were exchanging information. After a few moments Idris moved his head away. 'Sabre says Miss Audrina not in Enger-land,' he said. 'Sabre thinks she's still here.'

Rhiannon smiled. 'Sabre's wrong,' she told him. 'If she was here, somebody would have found her by now, wouldn't they?'

But Idris didn't seem to have heard. 'Still here,' he murmured, with conviction. 'Sabre *knows*.' There was a silence then. Idris seemed to be puzzling something in his mind while one hand gently stroked the horse's head. He looked at William again. 'Why *you* come here?' he asked.

William frowned, wondering how best to cut a long story short, but Rhiannon got there first.

'William is an orphan,' she explained. 'His parents . . . are gone. Like Mistress Audrina. Gone.' She made a gesture in the air, like a magician. 'So Mr Jessop says he can come and live with us here at the Rise.'

'Ah.' Idris nodded. He gave William a sympathetic look. 'William got no father or mother,' he said. 'Like Idris. All alone. Except for Sabre and Maggie and Dancer and Shadow.' He pointed to the horses in the stalls, one by one, as he named them. He paused, then seemed to think of something else. 'And my friend Rhiannon,' he added, pointing to her. 'She's not a horse, but she *is* my friend.'

William again struggled to keep a straight face. He waved a hand at the horses.

'Er . . . they are . . . nice animals,' he said. 'They look . . . strong . . . and healthy.'

Idris seemed more than happy to talk about them. 'Sabre is Mr Jessop's horse,' he said. 'Very proud, very fast he is. He is a stallion and he has Arab blood.' He nodded to the next in line. 'Maggie is Master Toby's horse. She is sweet-natured and gentle. Toby is supposed to ride her often, but he doesn't, so Idris takes her out instead.' He smothered a giggle with one hand as though he'd admitted to something naughty. Then he gestured to the two other horses. 'Dancer and Shadow pull the growler. Shadow had a bad leg, but Idris made a warm poultice and put it on her and she's fine now.'

William smiled. 'You...take good care of them,' he said.

'Yes.' Idris looked proud. 'Good care. Idris looks after his friends.'

There was an awkward silence then. Idris stood there, smiling vacantly at William, as though expecting a response, but William couldn't think of anything else to say.

'Well, we must go,' said Rhiannon. 'Mrs Craddock is waiting for us. But you've met William now and you know he's a friend. Right?'

'Will'yam a friend,' agreed Idris. 'Yes.'

'Perhaps we'll ask him to bring your food out to you

tonight?' suggested Rhiannon. 'So you can talk some more.' She glanced cautiously at William. 'Would that be all right?'

'Of course.' William hoped he sounded more confident than he felt.

'Good. Well, we'll be off then.' Rhiannon turned and headed for the doors and William went to follow her, but Idris ran suddenly forward to bar his way. 'Idris have present for new friend,' he said. He reached into the pocket of his breeches and pulled something out, which he pressed into William's hand. William stared at it in surprise. It was the skull of a large bird, he thought, a rook or a crow, something like that. He had no idea why Idris would have given it to him, but he didn't feel he could refuse it.

'Er... thank you,' he said, and he put the skull into his own pocket. 'That's... very nice of you.' He smiled in what he hoped was a friendly way, then stepped warily around Idris and followed Rhiannon out of the stable. As they headed back towards the house there was a sudden wild shout from behind them. Looking back, they saw Idris framed in the open window of the hayloft. He lifted a hand to wave and they waved back before walking on.

'What did he give you?' asked Rhiannon quietly.

William gingerly pulled the skull from his pocket to show her. She grimaced. 'He's very fond of those things,' she said. 'I'm not sure why. I expect he meant well.'

'What am I supposed to do with it?' asked William.

Rhiannon shrugged. 'He has a whole collection of them up in the hayloft,' she said. 'He tried to give me one once, but I told him I didn't really like bones.'

'I've been given some odd presents before, but never anything like this,' said William, slipping it back into his pocket.

'Well, anyway, he seems to have taken a shine to you. That's a good thing.' She smiled. 'He's an odd character, isn't he?'

William grinned. 'Oh, do you think so?' He laughed. 'What is his story?'

'Quite an interesting one,' said Rhiannon. 'I had it from Mrs Craddock when I first came here.'

'Go on,' William urged her.

'When he was only little, he was found sleeping in the hayloft one morning by the stableboys...This was in Mr Ransome's time, of course, when they had proper staff. Idris couldn't speak and nobody knew where he had come from, but he had these terrible scars on his back as though he had been beaten...' She scowled. 'How anybody could treat a young child like that, I do not know,' she said. 'At any rate, the stableboys took pity on him and fed him some of their rations and he started helping them around the place. They thought that they had better tell Mr Ransome about him, in case he didn't like a stranger being there. After a while he was able to speak again, but he would never tell them anything about where he had come from.'

'Makes sense, I suppose,' agreed William.

'For all that the old master was a soldier, he was said to be a kindly soul. He took pity on the child and announced that he could stay. The boy still hadn't spoken a word so Mr Ransome called him Idris, because he thought the name suited him. He even granted him a small wage for his trouble. Not that Idris ever did anything with the money. He had no use for it, you see. He only cares about horses... well, you saw how he was with Sabre...'

'It was almost as though they were speaking to each other!'

'Yes. I sometimes wonder if perhaps he really can do that. I know he *believes* he can, but that's not the same thing.' She frowned, shook her head. 'After the old master was gone, Idris devoted himself to Mistress Audrina. He thought the world of her, and I'm sure he wasn't happy when Mr Jessop started courting her and the two of them were married. But he stayed on here even after Mr Jessop came to live at the Rise. And then, when Mistress Audrina went missing... well, he hasn't stopped asking about her since.'

'You can tell he's still worried about her,' observed William.

'Oh, he frets about it! And it's been over a year now. Of course when Mr Jessop got rid of the other stable hands, Idris stayed on, even when they stopped giving him any pay. That suited Mr Jessop down to the ground... somebody who will work for a few scraps of food? Perfect!'

'And Idris is happy with that?'

'I don't think money means anything to him. He just loves living here, even though Toby teases him horribly sometimes. But then, you have to ask yourself, where else could he go? Who would employ him? He'd be a beggar wandering the streets. At least here he has a place to sleep and the company of the horses. We take him out a few leftovers every night and he seems healthy enough on it.'

William frowned. 'You know what he said about the riding crop? You don't think that Uncle Seth...?'

'Beats him?' Rhiannon blew air out between her pursed

lips. 'I'd say he wouldn't hesitate to beat anybody who didn't do exactly as he said. You mark my words, William, if he gives you an order, you obey it, to the letter. And don't waste time thinking about it.'

William looked at her. 'Rhiannon, he's never raised a hand to—'

'Me? Oh no. Not yet anyway. But I'd say I've come close once or twice. Whenever he thinks you are giving him an impudent look or being too slow in following orders, that's when you have to be careful. Especially if he's been drinking.'

'He drinks?'

'Yes. Oh, not often, but when he *does*, it's always to excess, and that's when the real meanness comes out of him. It's as though he's brooding on something and the drink brings it out. If you ever see him sitting alone with a bottle of wine, that's the time to make yourself scarce.'

'I'll keep that in mind,' said William.

They had come to the end of the path and Rhiannon reached out to open the door. William looked back across the garden towards the stables. Even at this distance he could make out Idris's gangling figure, framed in the window, watching. He tried to imagine what life must be like stuck out in the stable for days on end with hardly any human contact. William had thought that he had been dealt a poor hand, coming to this remote house, but today had been a reminder that there were others who were even worse off than him. And he decided, if Idris wanted to be his friend, then he would make sure he encouraged that friendship. He had a feeling he was going to need all the allies he could get.

Rhiannon opened the door and William followed her back into the house, where Mrs Craddock was waiting with more chores for them.

CHAPTER EIGHT
The First Month

The days passed by with surprising speed. Almost before William knew it, he had been at Jessop Rise for several weeks and had already fallen into a routine. Although it varied a little here and there, it still largely consisted of waiting on Toby's orders and, when he was not needed there, Mrs Craddock had a list of chores with which she could fill every available hour he had – resetting fires and carrying out the ashes, cleaning boots, scrubbing floors, chopping wood, beating the dust out of rugs slung over a washing line, fetching and carrying items of all shapes and sizes.

He would crawl into bed each night exhausted by his efforts, and happily his sleep was no longer interrupted by the sounds of crying, but still there persisted the feeling that he was being watched by some unseen presence; and there were little mysteries that he could never explain. On the second night at the house, for instance, he had placed the crow's skull that Idris had given to him on the table beside his bed, but when he woke the following morning it was on the floor beside his mattress. And this wasn't an isolated incident. When returning to his room each night, it was often to find that the skull was in a different place to where he had left it – over in a far corner of the room, inside the (thankfully empty) chamberpot, and once, after searching high and low for it, he finally discovered it tucked under the rough sacking of his pillow. Even on those occasions when the skull remained on the table, he was always convinced that it was facing in a slightly different direction to the way he had left it. It was disturbing.

There was another thing he couldn't explain. One morning, just before Mrs Craddock came rapping on his bedroom door, he woke suddenly to the sound of a scratching noise just above his head. His eyes focused and he found himself looking at the small dormer window, whose glass was frosted over. As he watched, transfixed, something on the other side of the glass scratched a perfect circle in the frost, making a soft rasping sound and he saw the faintest indication of a white fingertip pressed against the pane. He caught his breath. This was bewildering, because it would have required somebody to climb up onto that perilously sloping roof, but why would anybody take such a risk? William soon came to the realisation that it was a feat that was not within the powers of a human. There were several mornings that he woke to such a sight, but he decided not to mention it to anyone, knowing that they would only think him mad.

So he would simply dress himself and go down to the same, thankless breakfast of salty porridge, which he had now learned to tolerate, even though it was never going to be a favourite pleasure. Once his own meal was over with, he would fetch water and set fires until it was time to take Toby's breakfast up to his room. William quickly learned that you could never tell what kind of mood Toby would be in. When he was in a good humour, which was thankfully most of the time, he was pleasant company and always ready to share some of his food with William. Those were the good days. At other times he could be in a foul temper, and that was when William had to be wary of him, because on more than one occasion, after making a seemingly harmless remark, he came close to being, once again, on the receiving end of Toby's anger. It seemed to William that Toby had never got over the disappearance of his mother and it was generally a bad idea to mention her – nothing was more guaranteed to send him into a rage.

He was also seething with the knowledge that in a few year's time, on his twenty-first birthday, he would inherit the Ransome fortune – but until then Seth controlled every penny and Toby had to go cap in hand to ask for anything that he wanted – books, clothes, excursions, all of them things that Seth regarded as needless frivolities. Little wonder that Toby sometimes chose to flex his muscles by ordering the servants around or throwing his dinner plate at the wall if the cooking failed to meet his expectations. But underneath it all, William suspected there was a decent boy who had been through a bad time and had emerged scarred by the experience. He needed, more than anything else, to know the truth about what had happened to his mother.

As for Uncle Seth, William usually only set eyes on him at the evening meal, but where on his first night he had been invited to join his uncle and cousin, now he was expected to stand beside the table, dressed in his hall boy's coat, ready to top up glasses of wine, and to pass platters of food from one diner to the other. Occasionally one of them would make a churlish remark to him, telling him not to be so clumsy or to fill the glass up to the brim, but he was never again invited to sit down and eat with them. It was only after they had left the table that William had the brief opportunity to cram a few scraps into his mouth, before ferrying the remaining leftovers back to the kitchen, where Mrs Craddock waited, eagle-eyed.

Aside from at mealtimes, Uncle Seth kept himself to himself. He had a study at the back of the house where he would spend hours at a time and into which others, including Toby, could go only if they were invited. Occasionally Seth would emerge from his lair and hurry over to the stables, where he would instruct Idris to saddle up Sabre for him and he would gallop off, never saying where he was going or when he might be expected to return. Sometimes he could be gone for several days, without explanation, a state of affairs that riled Mrs Craddock, who seemed to think that Seth had left the house simply to make things more difficult for her. 'How is a soul supposed to run a house under such circumstances?' she would ask aloud, but if anybody had an answer to that, they kept it to themselves.

Mrs Craddock was a stern presence in the house, but William discovered that she did have a nicer side. As time went on, she began finding things around the place that she thought might be of use to him– an old oil lamp for his room, clothing that former staff had left behind which, like the hall boy's coat, she was able to take in, so that they were a better fit. She also came up with some proper bedding, an extra blanket and a decent nightshirt. These gifts were to be accepted quietly, because she hated any 'fuss' and probably didn't want it to get around that under that frosty exterior lurked somebody with a more thoughtful nature. Having said all that, she had a vicious tongue and never hesitated to scold William when he was slow or clumsy or forgetful.

The more that William got to know Rhiannon, the more he liked her. She was a sweet-natured, endlessly cheerful girl, who always seemed to make the best of her situation. If she had a failing, it was a tendency to believe in ghosts and goblins and all manner of superstitious nonsense. When William made the mistake of mentioning the strange business of the bird's skull to her, she was in no doubt as to whom the culprits were. 'The *Gwyllion*,' she told him, in a hushed voice. 'Little elves, they are. They love to come into houses and disrupt things. Don't worry, they are mostly harmless; they just like to make mischief.'

William had already learned not to laugh at her stories, as that was the one thing guaranteed to spoil her mood. She got these folk tales from her aged grandmother, who still lived in Porthmadog, and Rhiannon believed in them completely, so there was no point in arguing with her.

'*Gwyllion*, eh?' murmured William.

'You must never challenge them,' warned Rhiannon. 'If you do, they will wreck your room.'

William thought to himself that in his case, there was very little in there for them to spoil.

Idris too had become a friend, just as he had promised when he and William had first met, but it had to be said that it was a friendship like no other in the world. William and Rhiannon took turns to take a plate of food scraps out to the stables each evening, and upon receiving it he would always do the same thing: he would grab it from their hands and hurry up to the hayloft, where he would sit with his legs hanging out of the opening, cramming the food into his mouth as though afraid that somebody might attempt at any moment to take it from him. Making conversation with him was difficult to say the least; one never knew what subject might come into his head. He didn't so much talk as jabber about things, and if you ever asked him a direct question, it was unlikely that you'd get any kind of sensible reply. Mostly he liked to talk about the horses. Sabre, the haughty black Arab stallion, was clearly the finest horse here, but Maggie, the gentle roan mare, was his favourite. Since Toby rarely bothered to take her out of her stall these days, Idris would do it for him, riding her over the clifftops and into the wilds beyond, in search, no doubt, of more bones for his collection. From time to time, he would give one of his finds to William as another 'gift', and William always accepted, not wanting to hurt his feelings, so he began to acquire quite a collection. Idris made no secret of the fact that he generally preferred horses to people, but nonetheless William had come to believe that Idris was a true friend, somebody he could turn to in times of trouble. And for some reason a conviction lingered in William's mind that trouble *was* coming. He could feel it in his blood. And while he realised that this was as fanciful as one of Rhiannon's superstitious tales, still he was unable to shake the notion from his mind.

The last rays of October sunshine grew less powerful, the days shortened and the shadows lengthened as the new month exerted its chill grip on the land. Almost before William knew it, November had arrived and with it came the mists, drifting in off the sea to blanket the world in a hazy grey cloak.

And it was in November that more strange things began to happen.

PART TWO
November 1853

CHAPTER NINE
THE MUSIC BOX

William came suddenly awake to the pounding of a fist on his bedroom door. Mrs Craddock's strident voice informed him that it was six o'clock, his presence was required down in the kitchen and did he really intend to lie there all day?

'Get dressed and hurry down!' she barked. 'I've got plenty of jobs waiting for you!' Her heavy footsteps moved away along the landing.

'Coming,' he called, but he felt decidedly fuddled. The thumping on his door had interrupted his dream. He lay there a moment, trying to remember what it had been about, trying to piece together the broken shards like a dropped piece of pottery. Something to do with being outside, he thought, something to do with the beach and the grey sea pounding the sand while great flocks of crows soared and shrieked in the turbulent skies overhead ... he'd been digging in the sand beside a line of black rocks, creating a great damp pit that went down and down into darkness...

He looked over to the dormer window as he did every morning and, sure enough, once again there was a circle traced into the frosted glass as if by somebody's finger. But there was something different about it this morning. He sat up, looked closer and saw that in the centre of the ring two words were spelled out. He realised in amazement that they must have been written in reverse on the outside of the glass so that he could read them.

BRING HIM

William stared at the words, astonished and more than a little bit scared, as he tried to work out what they were supposed to mean. Bring *who*? And *where*?

It was no good. He couldn't put it all together and there was no time now. Bracing himself against the rush of cold air that he knew would greet him, he threw his blankets aside, shrugged off his nightshirt and dressed himself as quickly as he could. He glanced at the table and noticed that though the other skulls Idris had given him were there, the crow's skull, his first present, was not. He looked quickly around the room and could find no sign of it. He was half surprised when he slipped a hand into the pocket of his coat and found the smooth, hard skull resting in there. He sighed, shook his head, removed it from his pocket and set it back in its accustomed place on the table with the others. He glanced slowly around the room.

'Whoever you are,' he murmured, 'I really wish you'd make yourself known to me.'

It wasn't the first time he had expressed such a plea, but as ever there was no reply, just a long, unsettling silence. He told himself he was getting as bad as Rhiannon, believing in ghosts. But how else was he to account for it? Was it really the *Gwyllion*, Rhiannon's mischievous imps, creeping around the place after dark and playing foolish tricks on him? Somehow that idea seemed even less plausible than the antics of a spectre.

Well, he told himself, he had better get on. He hurried along the landing to the first flight of stairs. He went down them quickly but quietly, as Toby had instructed him. But as he turned to walk along the second-floor landing a strange thing happened. He drew near a door to a room, one that he passed every time he went up or down these stairs, a room to which the door had always been kept resolutely closed.

But this morning, as he came alongside it, there was a sharp click, the sound of a key turning in a lock; then the door handle was turned from within. William stopped in his tracks, not wanting to bump into whoever was about to step out of the room, but the door creaked slowly open to reveal . . . nobody. He caught sight of the foot of a four-poster bed, opulently dressed in colourful fabric . . . and then he became aware of the sound of music, a soft, tinkling melody playing from somewhere within.

'Hullo?' he said quietly, but there was no answer. He stepped closer and leaned forward to peer around the edge of the door, telling himself that there surely must be *somebody* in there, hidden behind the door; otherwise who could have turned the key? But no, the room appeared to be completely empty and he felt a strange chill lodge in the pit of his stomach. His instinct told him to get away from there as quickly as possible, to head down to the kitchen and get on with his work, but something in that lilting music lured him, made him want to identify the source of it. So he stepped warily over the threshold and soon discovered where the sounds were coming from. On a mahogany dressing table stood what looked like a small square music box, made from glossy black lacquered wood. The lid was up and a little automaton figure was dancing to the music, whirling around and around on a gilded pole. Fascinated, William moved closer, wanting to get a better look.

The figure was that of a dancer, a woman dressed in colourful gypsy-style clothes, a long black lace dress and bodice. She had curly black hair that hung to her shoulders, and her face was vividly painted, the cheeks rouged, the lips a bright cherry red, slightly parted to reveal twin rows of gleaming ivory teeth. One hand rested on her hip; the other, upraised, held a tiny tambourine, which clattered and rattled in time with the music. After watching entranced for several moments, William reached out and closed the lid of the box, shutting off the music.

It was suddenly very quiet in the room – perhaps, he thought, a little too quiet. He glanced around, reminding himself that the door had definitely been opened from the inside and yet there was nowhere here for a person to hide. Unless... he found himself beginning to stoop to look under the bed, but stopped himself, thinking that it was a ludicrous idea... Or was it simply that he didn't really want to see whoever might be hiding under there?

It occurred to him now that this was surely a woman's room. The air smelled faintly of lavender, and next to the music box stood a beautifully carved jewellery casket, its top open, the contents glittering enticingly. William reached out a hand to touch the jewels with his fingertips, tracing the shapes of the unfamiliar treasures – there were rings, brooches, necklaces, all manner of trinkets piled carelessly one atop the other, as though they were of no value whatsoever, but somehow their combined dazzle suggested that they surely must be worth a lot of money. He thought of the few small pieces of costume jewellery that his mother had owned and how his father had hung on to them after her death, keeping them in a little box. William wondered what had happened to them and had a sudden image of Mrs Selby standing before a mirror and trying on his mother's favourite necklace. He felt a terrible sadness fill him. He hadn't thought of his mother in years, and this was not how he wanted to remember her.

He stepped back from the dressing table, and as he did so a thick sheet of paper dropped down behind it, as though it had been hidden there, tucked into the gap between the table and the wall. Intrigued, William stooped and picked it up. It was a playbill printed on parchment, dated several years earlier and announcing in an ornate font: *Captain Tanner's Travelling Carnival,* which was to be found at 'The

Promenade, Harlech'. The bill promised a whole list of exotic acts, including Max the Strongman, the Flying Ravelli Brothers (a trapeze act) and the Amazing Carys, who danced something called the Tarantella and who had appeared all over the world. The parchment even featured an image of her, looking remarkably like the doll in the music box.

Unsure of what to do with the playbill, William turned away and carried it across to a small writing desk over by the single window. He set the bill down and glanced through the glass, to see that the garden was shrouded in thick mist as it had been for the past few days; he could see no more than a few feet into it. It would take the weak sun several hours to burn a way through that.

He transferred his gaze to what had already been lying on the surface of the desk. There were several sheets of thick writing paper, and beside them a decorative mahogany inkwell and a couple of metal-nibbed dip pens. William was about to turn away when he saw something he could scarcely credit. A black vertical line appeared at the left hand side of the topmost sheet of paper. As he watched, incredulously, the line swept down, then across to the right, then upwards with a graceful flourish to describe the letter H. He caught his breath and his eyes widened in disbelief.

As he stood there looking, the phantom hand continued to write, spelling out two words in elegant calligraphy.

Help Me

And then it hit him, what he had just witnessed – the sheer impossibility of it. He had a fleeting memory of those two words being spoken aloud in his room, the first night he arrived. He gasped, spun away in a panic and turned to hurry out of the room, only to find Uncle Seth standing in the open doorway, his expression one of dark fury.

'How in hell's name did you get in here?' he snarled.

William opened his mouth to reply, but for the moment all he could find was a jumble of half-formed words.

'Sir, I...I don't...I can't...the p...p...paper, it...'

But Seth pushed roughly past him to the writing desk and stood for a moment, staring down at the paper, his shoulders hunched. He grabbed the topmost sheet, turned and waved it at William.

'Did you write this?' he hissed.

'No, sir! No, I swear. It just...wrote itself.'

Now he picked up the playbill, an expression of horror on his face. 'And where...where did you get this?'

'It...it fell down from behind the—'

'You have been in my study, haven't you?' he growled. 'This is kept in a locked drawer in that room.'

William shook his head. 'Sir, I swear to you, it just—'

Seth took a threatening step closer. 'Do you think me a fool?' he sneered. 'Do you regard me as some kind of imbecile?'

'No, sir, I—'

'Then perhaps you'll tell me how you even come to be in here? A room that is kept locked at all times.'

'I...cannot explain it, sir. As I came by, the d-door... unlocked itself!'

'Unlocked itself?' Seth's eyes blazed with anger. 'We'll see about this,' he snarled. He folded the playbill and slipped it into his pocket, then crumpled the sheet of writing paper and flung it across the room. He stepped forward and grabbed William by the lapels of his coat, then dragged him out onto the landing, pausing only to slam the door behind him, with a crash that echoed through the house. He frogmarched William past the row of closed doors and down the next flight of stairs, William's feet flailing desperately to find purchase on the steps.

'Please, sir,' he begged, 'I can't...'

'Where did you get the key?' demanded Seth.

'I do not have one, sir!'

'Don't be ridiculous. How can the door be open if you do not have a key?'

The furore must have woken Toby. As they went past the door to his room, it opened and he peered out, tousle-headed and bleary-eyed, still dressed in his nightshirt and bedsocks.

'I say, what's going on?' he called out. 'What's William done?'

'Mind your own business,' snapped Seth. He pulled William down the final flight of stairs, with Toby trailing after them, and dragged him through the open door of the kitchen. Mrs Craddock and Rhiannon, engaged as ever in the preparation of food, looked up from the range in surprise.

'Mrs Craddock, perhaps you can explain how this boy came to be standing in Mistress Audrina's room?' bellowed Seth.

Mrs Craddock looked dismayed by the question. 'Why, I...I cannot, sir,' she told him. 'I have no idea how he came to be there.'

'Have I not given orders that the room is to be kept locked

at all times? That nobody is to go in there without my express permission?'

'Indeed you have, sir.'

'I also have reason to believe that he has been in my study.'

'That...that's not possible, sir.' She lifted the bunch of keys that hung on her belt and shook it. 'I alone go into that room, as arranged with you, to dust occasionally. And I always ensure that I lock the door after me. The same goes for Mistress Audrina's room.'

'Well then, either you forgot the last time you were there, or this boy has stolen the key from you. Which is it?'

There was a long silence. Mrs Craddock looked from William to Seth and back again. William felt he had to say something.

'Sir, I...I keep trying to tell you. As I came along the landing, the door opened...by itself...and there was music playing in there...a music box. I only went in to—'

He broke off with a yell of pain as Seth flung him bodily to the stone floor.

'And I tell you, boy, that I will tolerate no more lies! Say one more word to me now...just one, mark you, and you shall feel my riding crop across your breeches. Do you understand?'

William nodded miserably. How could he expect anyone to believe something that made no sense at all, least of all to him?

Seth took a step closer to Mrs Craddock. 'Well, woman,' he said, 'I'm waiting. Which is it? Did you forget or did he steal the key?'

Mrs Craddock shook her head. She sighed. 'He could not have taken the key,' she assured him. 'I keep it with me at all times.'

'Even when you sleep?'

'They are right beside my bed, sir. And I lock my door at night. So...'

'Yes?'

'So, I fear it...it must be *my* fault. I had thought I locked it after me the last time I was in there. Indeed I was sure I had. But...it would appear in this instance...that I was wrong.'

Seth nodded, a triumphant smile on his face. 'As I suspected,' he said. 'You, madam, will go straight up the stairs and secure that door. If such a thing ever occurs again, it will not go well with you, no matter how many years standing you have in this house, do you hear?'

'Yes, sir.'

'You shall be gone and a replacement found.' He looked down at William. 'And you, boy, will learn to keep your nose out of things that do not concern you.'

'Yes, sir,' murmured William. 'I'm sorry, sir.'

'And if I ever again hear you making up nonsense to explain your transgressions, you will be back in that workhouse before you have time to take another breath. Do I make myself clear?'

Again William nodded. 'Yes, sir.'

Seth glared at Mrs Craddock. 'Well, woman, what are you waiting for? A written invitation?'

Mrs Craddock waved a hand at the cooking range. 'If you please, sir, the porridge...?'

'I'll see to it,' said Rhiannon, stepping briskly to the pot to continue stirring. Mrs Craddock nodded gratefully and went past Seth to the door, causing Toby to step aside to let her pass. Seth stood for a moment, glowering down at William before he too turned on his heel and strode away. Toby waited a few moments to ensure that his stepfather was out of earshot before entering the kitchen. He looked down at William and chuckled delightedly.

'What on earth have you been up to, cousin?' he inquired. 'I haven't seen Seth so incensed in a long while.'

William got carefully to his feet, aware now that one knee and one elbow were stinging where he'd grazed them on the stone flags. 'I didn't even know I wasn't allowed to go in there,' he said miserably. He hobbled over to the kitchen table and sat down.

'He's very particular about that room,' said Rhiannon, as she frantically stirred the porridge. She glanced quickly around and lowered her voice. 'He has been ever since Mistress Audrina went missing. He doesn't like anyone to set foot in there.'

Toby wandered over and took the seat beside William. 'You're lucky he didn't tan your hide,' he said. And then he chuckled. 'What larks!'

'I'm glad I was able to entertain you,' said William resentfully.

'Oh, don't be like that!' said Toby, who seemed in one of his better moods today. 'He'll calm down soon enough. He's always crotchety first thing in the morning. That's one of the reasons I prefer to get up late.' He lifted a hand to run his fingers through his tousled hair. 'So how *did* you manage to sneak in there? I've wanted to have a look many a time, but I've never been allowed the key.'

William looked at Toby warily. 'You won't believe me if I tell you,' he said. 'You'll lose your temper.'

'No, I won't.'

'You promise?'

'Of course. You have my word as a gentleman.'

William wasn't particularly reassured, but decided to risk it. He told Toby and Rhiannon exactly what had happened, although for reasons he wasn't quite sure of, he omitted the part about the writing on the paper. If anything was guaranteed to make Toby angry, it was that.

'I remember that dancer,' said Toby. 'Seth brought it back from a business trip a year or so ago. It was a present for my mother. It's strange because he was never much of a one to buy gifts, but something about that had caught his eye, he said. My mother loved it.'

'But what do you make of the door unlocking itself?' prompted William.

'You heard Mrs Craddock,' said Toby. 'I expect she forgot to secure it last time she was in there. Your feet on the floorboards probably caused the door to pop open. No great mystery there.'

'And the music box, playing when I went in?'

Toby shrugged. 'Probably Mrs Craddock again. I would venture she had a look at it when she was cleaning the room and simply forgot to lower the lid.'

'But . . . don't you have to wind a thing like that with a key?' William looked at Rhiannon. 'When was she last in there?'

'Days ago,' said Rhiannon. 'Anyway, I know who is responsible.'

William and Toby looked at her with interest. 'Who?' said Toby.

'The *Gwyllion*,' she said dramatically.

'The what?' cried Toby.

'They are mischievous elves,' explained William wearily. 'They play tricks on people.'

'Ah,' said Toby. He closed his eyes. 'I had forgotten Rhiannon and her little folk tales.' He thought for a moment. 'So these Gwilly . . . whatever you call them, they can unlock doors, can they?'

'They don't need to. They can make themselves flat and slide under the gap beneath.'

Toby sniggered. 'That would be a handy thing to master. There's a few rooms in this house I wouldn't mind taking a look inside.'

'Such as?' asked Rhiannon.

'Seth's study, for one. He spends hours in there and I'm never allowed to put my nose inside. I'd love to know what occupies him for so long. And my mother's room of course. I'd like to look for clues as to what made her run away. But Seth is always adamant that nobody is allowed in there any more.' He looked at William. 'What was it like?'

'As though it had just been left,' said William. 'All of her jewellery was still lying around. And the room smelled of lavender.'

'My mother's favourite perfume,' murmured Toby. 'I remember it well.' He sighed. 'Perhaps I should ask Mrs Craddock to lend me the key some time, so I can have a crafty look.'

'I wouldn't if I were you,' Rhiannon advised him. 'You saw what happened to William.'

Just then Mrs Craddock stalked back into the room, a cross expression on her ruddy face. 'I don't know who is playing silly devils in this house, but it has to stop,' she growled. They all turned to look at her.

'Whatever do you mean?' asked Toby.

'I went straight back to the room,' she said. She moved over to the range and took over the stirring of the porridge.

'Somebody must think they're very funny,' she added, sprinkling in another spoonful of salt, 'but I'll find out who it is, you mark my words.'

'Mrs Craddock, you're not making very much sense,' said Toby.

She turned to look at him. 'When I got up there,' she said, 'the door was already locked.'

CHAPTER TEN
ANOTHER MYSTERY

At dinner that evening Seth was in an unusually good mood and William's misadventure of earlier seemed to have been forgotten. This might have been encouraged by Seth's having already drunk a couple of glasses of red wine before Mrs Craddock and Rhiannon had even brought the steaming platters of food to the table – but William remembered what Rhiannon had said about his uncle's drinking, so he resolved not to say anything that might upset him. He waited on Seth and Toby as usual, but Seth seemed to want to include him in the conversation and even invited him to help himself to the odd morsel, which was quite unlike him. William, always hungry, wasn't going to let the chance go by without taking advantage of it – but he also knew not to take too much, because Seth's moods were as changeable as the weather; help himself to too big an item and William might find himself on the wrong end of a vengeful fist. So he reined himself in, taking only the odd mouthful here and there.

'So, nephew, how are you settling in at Jessop Rise?' Seth asked, as he gulped down a mouthful of meat, and William told himself it was probably best to steer well clear of the truth. He wasn't about to tell his uncle that he was being plagued by ghostly visions and inexplicable happenings. 'Come along, boy,' Seth prompted him. 'You've been here over a month now. How are things?'

'I'm settling in well, uncle, thank you for asking,' said William, hiding his true feelings behind a fake smile.

'Hear that, Toby?' Seth chuckled, casting a sidelong look at his stepson. 'Impeccable manners, your cousin, don't you think?'

Toby shrugged. As ever at such times, he was devoting most of his concentration to polishing off the contents of a plate that was piled high with food.

'He's just making sure he stays on your good side,' he muttered, through a mouthful of meat.

'Well, that's more than you ever do,' observed Seth. 'You seem to devote your life to vexing me.' He swallowed another mouthful of wine. 'I was thinking that we should pay a visit to the quarry tomorrow,' he added. 'We haven't been up there in a while and it's good for the men's morale, to put in an occasional appearance. Keeps them on their toes.'

Toby looked distinctly uninterested. 'Can't we wait for better weather?' he asked. 'It's freezing outside.'

'Nonsense!' barked Seth. 'It'll do you good to get some fresh air in your lungs. The trouble with you is that you spend too much time in front of the fire, reading those blasted books.'

'A good book can take you anywhere,' argued Toby, his chin shiny with pork fat. 'There are novels that can take you out of this dreary world and plunge you into dark, exciting places...'

'Sounds exactly like the quarry,' said Seth, and he laughed at his own poor joke. 'Perhaps we'll dangle you by a rope from one of the galleries, Toby, since you're so fond of dangerous adventures.' He finished his drink and waved the empty glass at William for a refill. William picked up the jug from the table and topped it up to the brim. He had already learned that Seth always complained if he thought he'd been given a half-measure. 'Perhaps we should invite William along,' suggested Seth, 'so he can witness the kind of industry that pays for the roof over his head. What do you think of that idea, nephew?'

'Sir, I would like that very much,' said William, and he genuinely meant it. In the whole month, the only times he'd been able to step out of the house were when he was sent out for water or to take Idris his evening scraps.

'That's settled then. We'll set off straight after breakfast. I'll have Idris harness up the growler. We'll ride over there in style.' He looked at William. 'Go and tell Mrs Craddock that she needs to have a light breakfast ready for eight o'clock.' He turned his head to give Toby a certain look. 'That means you'll need to heave your fat carcass out from under the covers by seven. You can take your morning meal at the table with me for a change.'

Toby scowled at this. 'Seven o'clock?' he complained. 'It'll barely be light by then.'

Seth shook his head. 'It'll do you good. You need to get into the habit of rising early, lad. Or do you think you can continue with your indolent ways when you are master of this house?'

'When I'm master, I'll do as I damn well please,' muttered Toby.

As William left the room, it was to the sound of Seth's voice, suddenly louder and sounding much less pleasant than it had before.

In the kitchen, Rhiannon was just putting on her shawl, ready to make the long walk down the cliff path to Porthmadog village, while Mrs Craddock busied herself at the range, kneading the dough for the next day's bread.

'Mrs Craddock, can you have breakfast ready for Mr Jessop and Master Toby for eight o'clock tomorrow?' William asked her.

'I dare say I can,' she said. 'What's come over Master Toby? I've never known him put a toe out of bed at that time of the day.'

'He and Mr Jessop are going to the quarry,' William explained. 'I'm to go with them,' he added excitedly. 'Uncle Seth is going to show me the place.'

Mrs Craddock chuckled. 'You just be careful you don't get too close,' she told him. 'It's a dangerous place, that quarry. Seems as if every other day there's somebody killed by falling rocks and the like.' She looked suddenly wistful. 'That's what happened to my Elwyn,' she said.

William looked at her in surprise. He had never thought to ask if there was or ever had been a *Mr* Craddock. 'Your...husband?' he ventured.

She nodded. 'He worked at the quarry,' she said. 'Oh, it was years ago, mind. We were only young. I was the scullery maid yure, doing the same job as Rhiannon does now, and Elwyn worked as a quarryman for your grandfather. Me and Elwyn had been married not much more than a year...' As she talked her hands continued to work the floury dough on the worktop in front of her, but her eyes were focused on something in the distance, something only she could see. 'It was the middle of summer, I remember, a beautiful sunny day. I was pegging out washing on the line in the garden and a young boy came running towards the house, and the moment I saw him I knew...I knew what had happened. The boy was all out of breath, but he told me, he said that Elwyn had suffered a fall. He'd been working in the gallery, you see...that's what they call the rock face – the gallery. His rope had snapped and he'd fallen the full height of the quarry onto the rocks below. Killed instantly, he was. He didn't suffer, which is a blessing. But...oh, when I saw what was left of his body...' She broke off for a moment, her eyes filling with tears. She picked up a cloth and dabbed at them. 'That was it for me,' she said brusquely. 'There was never anybody else I was interested in. He was my world, that man. Once he was gone, there didn't seem much point in anything, but I put my head down and got on with things. Well, you do, don't you? We had no children, either.

That was something we'd thought would come one day, but...it was not to be...' Her voice trailed away and she seemed to realise that she had just told William much more than she had ever intended to. 'Anyway,' she said, 'all that was years ago. What's done is done and can never be changed.'

'Oh, Mrs Craddock...' William felt terrible. Why had he never thought to ask her about her life? 'I...I didn't know,' he said.

'Of course not,' she said, waving a floury hand. 'How could you? Rhiannon knows about it though, don't you, girl?' Rhiannon nodded gravely. 'So all I'm saying, William, is don't you be taking any risks while you're at the quarry. That place is to be treated with respect.'

'I'll be careful,' he assured her. 'Mrs Craddock, can I...?'

'Can you what?'

'Can I have my porridge before I go?' He felt bad asking such a silly little question after what he'd just been told, but he thought, not as bad as if he went off for the day with an empty belly.

'We'll see if I have time,' she told him, but the half-smile on her face suggested to him that she would make sure he was fed before he left.

'Well, I'd best be off,' said Rhiannon, a little too loudly. As she turned to face William, he noticed something hanging around her neck on a length of chain: a brown, furry thing, no bigger than a man's thumb.

'What's that?' he asked, intrigued.

'It's my rabbit's foot,' she told him. 'My mother got it for me. It's supposed to be a lucky charm.'

William chuckled. 'Well, I don't know if I'd put much faith in that,' he said. 'The rabbit had four legs and none of them seem to have brought *him* much luck!'

'Don't you be making fun now,' Mrs Craddock chided him. 'Rhiannon needs something to keep her safe going down that cliff road in the dark. Especially in all this fog. And there's nothing so good as a fresh rabbit's foot. In most houses in Porthmadog, every newborn baby has its head brushed with a rabbit's foot for luck.' She smiled at the girl. 'You take your time now. Don't be in a rush to get back to your mother.'

'I won't,' she said.

'William, unless they're expecting you back in the dining room, you can take Idris out his scraps and tell him about tomorrow morning. Mind, he's not able to tell the time, and anyway he doesn't have a clock, so just tell him to be ready when the sun comes up. He'll understand that.'

William nodded. He collected the bowl of food scraps from its place by the door and he and Rhiannon went out through the scullery to the back of the house. He was momentarily shocked by how thick the fog was.

'Will you be all right?' he asked Rhiannon.

'Don't worry about me,' she told him. 'I could walk that path blindfolded.'

He smiled at that. 'Poor Mrs Craddock,' he murmured. 'I didn't know about her husband.'

Rhiannon nodded. 'Sometimes when people are old,' she said, 'you forget that they were young once. You think they've always been the age they are now. She told me one time that she was a pretty thing when she was young. Turned all the boy's heads, she said.'

They stood looking at each other for a moment and then both of them started laughing at exactly the same moment. Somehow it seemed so unlikely.

'I'll see you tomorrow morning,' said Rhiannon, and she turned and walked around the side of the house towards the front gate. William watched her go, feeling strangely protective of her. He didn't like to think of her walking down that lonely road in the dark. After just a few steps she was lost in the fog.

Remembering that he had food to deliver, he started along the garden path. The fog was too thick for him to make out the shape of the stables, but he veered to his right when he thought he had gone far enough and moved forward, his feet crunching in the frozen grass. For what seemed a very long time he saw nothing, and he was just on the verge of readjusting his angle, when the stables loomed out of the all-surrounding grey cover. He could just see a dim wash of light spilling from the open doorway. 'Idris?' he called as he walked inside. An oil lamp stood on a barrel, painting the interior with a dull yellow glow. 'Idris, I've brought your supper!'

A moment later a head appeared in the opening of the hayloft, lengths of straw stuck in the unruly thatch of hair. William knew that now the weather was turning colder, Idris spent much of his time bundled up in a thick covering of hay, which he always claimed was warmer than any eiderdown. Spotting the bowl in William's hand, he leaped from the loft onto the ground below, performing his usual ungainly forward roll. Once upright, he bounded over to William and snatched the food out of his hand. Before William could say anything, he had run back to the ladder and clambered quickly up, taking his usual seat in the opening of the loft, with his legs hanging over the side.

He sniffed at the bowl appreciatively. 'Good!' he said and started to cram the food into his mouth with his fingers. It was nobody's idea of a nice meal, an odd collection of stale crusts, pieces of fat and gristle and whatever else had been salvaged from other diner's plates throughout the day, but Idris never complained and always devoured everything he was given. While he ate, William clambered halfway up the ladder until they were close enough to talk.

'How are you, Idris?' he asked.

'Idris is good. Not hungry no more.'

William nodded. 'Mr Jessop wants you to take him to the quarry tomorrow,' he said. 'In the growler. I'm coming along too.'

Idris looked delighted at this news. 'Good! I get to wear form!' he said.

'Form?' echoed William, bemused.

'Form!' Idris nodded excitedly and, reaching behind him into the straw, he pulled out a shabby-looking brown jacket with fraying red epaulettes and tarnished brass buttons. 'Idris's form,' he said proudly. 'Make Idris look like a proper servant.'

'Oh, your *uni*form,' William corrected him.

'Yes, form!' agreed Idris, talking through a mouthful of

143

food. 'That's the word. Makes Idris look handsome.'

'I didn't know you had one!'

'Only allowed to wear it in the growler,' he said. 'Mr Jessop says so. One time Idris wears it in the stable and Mr Jessop sees. He brings out the riding crop.' He mimed the action of an arm rising and falling. 'Idris remembers after that,' he said. He looked down towards the gloomy stalls and made a loud snorting sound, blowing air out in a way that made his lips vibrate. A couple of answering calls came back out of the gloom. 'Shadow and Dancer are happy,' he said. 'We've not taken out the growler in a while.'

'But... how do they know?' asked William.

'Idris just told them!' He crammed a chunk of meat into his mouth, then half choked on a large piece of gristle and had to tilt his head back to swallow it down. He coughed, spluttered, cleared his throat. 'When do we go?' he asked.

'Be ready when the sun comes up,' said William, pointing towards the ceiling. 'You understand? Sunrise?'

Idris nodded. The small earthenware bowl was empty now. His fingertips traced the bottom of it, searching for morsels he might have missed. But there was nothing. He sighed and handed the empty bowl back to William. Then he let out a long, satisfied belch. 'Good food,' he said.

'Did you go out today?' William asked him.

'Oh yes,' said Idris. 'On Maggie. We ride over the clifftops.' He rummaged in the straw behind him and pulled something out. 'Idris find this for you,' he said, pressing it into William's hand. It was another skull, a rat or a vole, William thought, something else to add to his rapidly expanding collection.

'Thank you,' he said brightly. 'That's a nice one.' He could never think of much else to say at such times. He slipped it into his pocket. 'Did you go far?' he asked.

Idris mimed the action of holding a set of reins. 'We ride for miles and miles!' he announced gleefully. 'Then we see Mr Jessop riding Sabre, but Mr Jessop doesn't see Idris. Idris hides in the trees. Idris thinks if Mr Jessop sees him on Maggie, he will bring out the riding crop again.'

William frowned. 'Where was this?' he asked.

'The old chapel,' said Idris. He reached into his mouth with a finger and tried to prise something from between his teeth.

'What's the old chapel?'

'A church. All fallen down now. No roof.'

'I wonder what he was doing there,' mused William. 'He always seems to be riding off to different places.'

'Who?' asked Idris, looking mystified.

'Uncle Seth!'

'Ah! Idris knows. Idris *sees* what he is doing. But Mr Jessop doesn't see Idris, because Idris hides.' He seemed very pleased with himself for some reason.

'So . . . what *was* he doing?' asked William.

'Hmm?'

William rolled his eyes. 'Uncle Seth – what was he doing?'

'Ah! Mr Jessop goes to the stone . . . the *big* stone . . .' He gestured with his hands, making a boxlike shape. 'The place where people kneel?'

'The . . . altar?'

'Yes! The all-tar. Mr Jessop takes out a box from under the all-tar. He opens it and looks inside. And then . . . then . . .'

'Yes?' prompted William.

'Then he kneels down and prays.' Idris put his own hands together, as though he thought that perhaps William was unfamiliar with the term. 'Like this.'

This didn't seem to make sense to William. Seth had never done or said anything that would make William think of him as a religious man; indeed, quite the opposite. And if he *was* religious, why go to an old ruined chapel to pray, rather than the one in Porthmadog that Rhiannon had told him about?

'Mr Jessop talks to himself,' added Idris. 'The whole time.'

'Really?'

'Oh yes. And then Idris can see his shoulders are moving up and down.'

'What do you mean?'

'Idris can see ... that Mr Jessop is crying.'

CHAPTER ELEVEN
JESSOP QUARRY

Idris clicked his tongue and urged the two horses onwards as they pulled the heavy carriage up the steep slope of the hillside. William sat on the uncomfortable wooden bench beside Idris, clinging on for dear life. He had not been invited to ride in the relative comfort of the upholstered interior with Seth and Toby.

'Nearly there,' Idris announced with a grin. 'Nearly there, Will'yam.' He was dressed in his coachman's outfit. The long brown tailcoat with its ragged braiding had clearly been made for a much stouter person than he, and even the mildewed leather boots he wore looked somehow far too big for him, his skinny legs emerging like a pair of broom handles, but he was in his element this morning, urging the horses along with snorts and whinnies, which they seemed to respond to.

It was a bright clear morning and they had been travelling for perhaps half an hour. The route had taken them across

148

the clifftops and down through Porthmadog in the neigh-
bouring valley, past rows of little stone cottages with
thatched roofs and smoky chimneys. Only a few solitary
women were in the streets this morning, fetching water from
the pump in the square or visiting the little general store for
provisions. The coach passed by a low building with a
thatched roof and William saw a painted wooden sign
hanging above the door: 'The Quarryman's Arms'.

'That's the tavern,' Idris told him. 'That's where the men
go to drink their ale. Has Will'yam ever drunk ale?'

'No,' said William. 'Have you?'

'One time,' said Idris. 'One time Master Toby gave Idris
some ale. He made Idris drink three tankards really fast.'
Idris grimaced. 'Then Idris is sick everywhere,' he muttered.
'Idris will never do that again!'

William shook his head. 'That wasn't very nice of him,' he
observed.

'Sometimes Master Toby likes to play tricks,' said Idris
woefully.

The coach rattled on along the narrow street. William
couldn't help but notice that, as it went by, each woman they
passed bowed her head respectfully and stood still until it
had gone on its way, as though greeting the carriage of

a king. William began to appreciate the power that Seth Jessop had in these parts and only then did it dawn on him why there were no men to be seen. They would all be up at the quarry, working for their daily bread.

Once they had left Porthmadog the land rose steadily again in a series of increasingly steep inclines until they finally came to this last, vertiginous hill; at Idris's insistence the horses redoubled their efforts and the carriage finally crested the ridge. 'Whoa!' said Idris, and he pulled the horses to a halt.

'There it is . . .'

William had his first view of Jessop Quarry, and the sight of it nearly snatched his breath away. He didn't know what he'd been expecting, but certainly not this.

Directly below him, and for miles in every direction, not a blade of grass nor a tree nor a bush existed. There was nothing but great jagged heaps of dark grey slate, piled high in no apparent order; between these hellish mounds, narrow train tracks ran along a steep incline to left and right, and on those tracks wagons rolled downhill, heavily laden with slate blocks or, empty of freight, were pulled back up again by teams of ponies. From this height the wagons looked like children's toys, dwarfed by the immensity of their surroundings, but it was not the wagons that captured William's gaze, nor the towering mounds of slate on every side of them.

It was what lay in the very centre of his vision – the quarry itself.

It was a great ragged scar in the landscape, an open wound, looking for all the world as though a giant had reached down and scooped a massive handful of rock out of the earth. On three sides the opening was a sheer drop, and as William's gaze focused he became aware of tiny shapes on the walls of the quarry, puny moving figures suspended on lengths of rope, swinging from side to side or moving up and down in a series of leaps and hops. It took him another moment to realise that these were actually men, clinging like insects to the rock face as they worked with levers to break free huge chunks of slate. As William watched, something high up on the right-hand side of the rock face began to move, and suddenly a massive block of slate detached itself and came tumbling down, end over end, until it hit the floor of the quarry in a cloud of dust. Below it, other tiny figures scrambled nimbly out of harm's way and then, once the block had settled, converged back on it, like ants gathering around a discarded apple core.

Finally the delayed sound of the impact drifted up to William, a low rumbling crash that reverberated around the surrounding hills.

'So, what do you think of my little enterprise?' asked a voice behind him, and he turned to see that Seth was leaning out of the open window of the growler, smiling up at him.

'It . . . it's incredible,' murmured William. 'I had no idea.'

'Beats your father's cotton mill into a cocked hat, don't you think?'

William didn't quite know how to answer that. 'Well, it's . . . certainly very *different*,' he admitted. 'At the mill it was all machinery, and here—'

'A hundred and fifty skilled men,' interrupted Seth. 'More come every day looking for a position. And shall I tell you the sweetest part? Each one of them pays me a fee, just for the right to be allowed to work here. Before they have split a single block, before they have so much as climbed a rope, their money is in my pocket. What do you think of that, boy?'

William wasn't sure what to think. It sounded to him like a ridiculous arrangement. He had no idea how much his father had been paid to work at the cotton mill in Northwich, but he was pretty sure he hadn't had to buy his way into the place.

'So . . . how do the men make any money?' he asked.

'They have to work very, very hard,' said Seth. 'If at the end of the month they've made enough roofing slates to earn back the amount they've already paid, only then do they start to move into profit.'

'And if they don't make enough slates?'

'Then their children go hungry.' Seth smiled contentedly. 'So you see, it's an excellent system. They have every incentive to work hard.'

'It sounds . . . complicated,' said William, but the word he really wanted to use was 'wrong'.

'Yes, well, this will be where *you'll* end up if you don't keep on your toes,' said Seth. It was probably meant as a joke but there was no sign of any humour in his eyes.

'I'll do my best not to disappoint you, sir,' said William, who had already learned that it made good sense to always tell his uncle exactly what he wanted to hear.

'Ride on, Idris,' said Seth, and he ducked his head back into the coach. Idris flicked the reins and the horses started on their way again, moving more easily now the route was taking them downhill. They slowly descended the road, which was laid out in a series of zigzags, and as they moved steadily closer, William began to take in more details.

He could now see a long, low stone building and a great waterwheel standing beside it, which was being driven by a fast-moving stream that flowed past the entrance to the quarry. He could see the winding house with its giant wooden drums spooling in the metal cables as they dragged the heavy wooden palettes, laden with rough slates, up the steep incline that led out of the quarry. Everywhere there was dust and noise and the staccato rattle of metal chisels on stone. William was sure of one thing: he didn't ever want to work here. It looked like a very hard life.

As Idris pulled the growler into a flat space in front of the winding house, a stocky man in overalls detached himself from a group of workmen and hurried over to meet them.

'Here comes Huw Rhys Griffiths,' said Idris, and when William gave him a blank look, he added, 'Rhiannon's father.'

Huw was a short but tough-looking man, dressed in dirt-plastered overalls, his grubby face dominated by a bristling moustache. He strolled up, nodded to Idris and then reached out to open the door of the carriage. 'Mr Jessop,' he said, touching the peak of his flat cap. 'And here's Master Toby! I wasn't expecting to see you two today.'

'Precisely why we came,' said Seth, climbing out and looking imperiously around. 'Warning your workers that you're going to put in an appearance would be a ridiculous thing to do, don't you think?'

'I . . . suppose so, sir.'

Just then a man strode past the coach, a heavy-set fellow wearing a brightly coloured red scarf. As he walked by, he and Seth exchanged a look, and from his vantage point up on the seat, William thought he saw the man nod his head slightly in Seth's direction. Seth nodded back and the man walked on towards the quarry. Then Seth turned and looked irritably into the carriage. 'Well, come along, Toby, move yourself. Or have you taken root in there?'

Toby edged towards the doorway, but his glum expression suggested he would much rather remain where he was. Despite the fact that he was all bundled up in a heavy overcoat and a rather comical-looking top hat, he kept his arms wrapped around himself as though he had suddenly found himself in the Arctic. 'Can't I stay here?' he asked. 'It's freezing out there.'

'It is not freezing,' Seth corrected him. 'It is brisk, that's all. And you have enough layers on you to hold off the deepest winter. Oh, come along, boy; I want you out here now.'

Toby complied, huffing and puffing as he eased himself down from the carriage. Seth turned back to Huw. 'So, how are things progressing?' he asked.

'Well, enough, Mr Jessop, well enough. We're running around the clock. Unfortunately we had another accident earlier this week. A man called—'

'I'm not interested in accidents,' snapped Seth, cutting him short. 'How is the productivity?'

'On the rise, sir, as predicted. Miss Treadle in the office has all the ledgers up to date for you. I think you'll find that—'

'I'll let Miss Treadle explain all that,' said Seth. 'We shall go into the office, you and I, and have a thorough look at the paperwork.'

'Very good, sir.'

Seth looked at Toby. 'You two can stay out here,' he said. 'Get yourselves some fresh air. Toby, I want you to take the opportunity to escort your cousin around the quarry.'

'Do I have to?' sighed Toby.

'Yes, you do! Show him your eventual inheritance. And make sure you take him up to look at the gallery. Get in close, the two of you. I'm sure he'll be interested to see how it works.'

'Must we?' murmured Toby.

'What's the matter?' Seth asked him. 'Scared of getting too close?'

'Not at all.'

'I suppose you'd be happier sat at home, reading one of your books. A far less risky prospect. Of course, if you're too nervous...'

'I'm not,' Toby insisted, looking exasperated. 'It's nothing to do with nerves. It's just that I've seen it a hundred times.'

'And your cousin hasn't! Now, are you going to show him?'

'Yes, yes, whatever you say.'

'I'm glad to hear it. Be off with you. I'll come and find you when I'm finished.' Seth and Huw strode off towards a small stone building next to the winding house as William climbed down from his seat to join Toby. 'Where shall we start?' he asked.

Toby gave him a withering look. 'You *really* want to see it?' he asked in disbelief.

'Of course I do,' said William. 'It looks interesting.'

Toby smirked. 'You're a hopeless case, aren't you?' he said. 'You'll be telling me next that you went to look at the factory where your father worked.'

'I did,' admitted William. 'He even let me have a go at one of the looms.'

'Lucky old you,' sneered Toby. He sighed. 'Oh well, come along then. I suppose walking will at least help to warm us up a bit.'

'What shall *I* do, Master Toby?' asked Idris.

Toby looked up at him. 'You can go to hell as far as I'm concerned,' he said uncharitably, but when Idris looked as though he might actually be considering the best way of getting there, he added wearily, 'Just wait here with the horses.' He started off towards the quarry and William followed him.

'The man's an idiot,' muttered Toby.

'Oh, I believe he's wiser than you think,' said William. 'There's nothing he doesn't know about horses.'

'Which is precisely why he'll never amount to anything. Can you imagine being content with the company of animals?'

William shrugged. 'They're nicer than some people you meet,' he said.

Toby gave him an odd look, as though he suspected he might be included in that comment. He gestured around with a broad sweep of an arm. 'Well, this is it,' he said,

'Jessop Quarry. One day it will all be mine. The whole noisy, stinking lot of it.'

'You sound as though you hate it,' observed William.

'Oh, I don't wish to sound ungrateful. I like what it can *buy*. I like the fact that I'll never have to break my back doing the kind of thing that they are doing –' he pointed in the direction of the sweating, labouring men hanging from the gallery – 'but if I'm really honest, I don't much like what my stepfather has done with the business.'

'How do you mean?'

'Well, as anyone who knows the industry will tell you, he pays the quarrymen a pittance and works them into early graves. And the truth is, there's really no need for it.'

'Perhaps you'll be able to change that when the quarry is yours?'

Toby frowned. 'I suppose. But that isn't going to happen any time soon.'

'I thought when you were twenty-one, you'd—'

'No, no, that's the house and the estate. I won't inherit the quarry until Seth dies, or decides to pass it on to somebody else.' He shrugged. 'Not that I'm particularly bothered. He's welcome to it. It's not what I would choose as a business for myself.'

'What *would* you choose?' wondered William.

Toby considered for a moment. 'I should like to be a writer,' he announced grandly.

'A writer?'

'Yes. An author. I should like to write wonderful adventure novels and great plays and have people all over the world admire my work.'

'I see. Are you... any good at writing?'

Toby shrugged. 'I've never really tried,' he admitted. 'But let's face it, how hard can it be?'

William suspected that it might be a very difficult thing to do, but realised that Toby wouldn't want to hear that, so he pointed off to his left to where a row of wagons packed with wooden boxes was rattling downhill between the heaps of discarded slate. 'Where's that thing going?' he asked.

'To the dock at Porthmadog,' said Toby. 'That's what's called a dandy wagon, and those boxes contain finished roofing slates. They'll be sent off to France, Germany, Holland... all sorts of places. Our slates are prized over there, you know. People in Wales seem to think they're too damned expensive, so most of our output goes abroad. The French believe they're the finest slates that money can buy and they're willing to pay just about any price for them.'

'And what are all those big grey hills?'

'That's just the slag,' said Toby. 'The waste.' When William still looked puzzled he explained. 'For every ton of slate we use, there's thirty tons of wastage. It has to go *somewhere*.'

'That seems a lot,' observed William. 'Can't it be used for something?'

'No. It's just odds and ends...pieces with flaws in them...bits that have broken off when the blocks were being sawn. Useless stuff. I expect it will lie there for years...centuries, I shouldn't wonder.'

They walked on and Toby continued to point things out. 'Those are the saw houses, where the big slates are cut to a manageable size,' he explained. 'And then they are carried here to the splitters.' They had come to an open-sided wooden shed, where rows of men in leather aprons were seated at benches, each man splitting oblong pieces of slate with a hammer and chisel. As William watched, entranced, a worker skilfully separated an already thin sheet of slate again and again with a few deft taps of the hammer, to produce six perfect roof slates. These were stacked in a corner, and a couple of skinny young lads of around William's age systematically gathered them up and carried them outside, to be stored in wooden boxes. 'Those lads are called the *rybelwrs*," said Toby. 'That's what you'll be doing if Seth ever decides to send you here.'

'You don't think he will, do you?' asked William anxiously.

Toby sniggered. 'What's wrong, cousin?' he asked. 'I thought you said it was "interesting"?'

'That doesn't mean I'd like to work here. It looks punishing.'

'I'm sure it won't come to that,' said Toby. 'I imagine if Seth was planning to send you, he'd have done it by now. He's not one to waste time, my stepfather.'

'Do you . . . do you *like* him?' asked William, and a fleeting expression crossed Toby's face, a kind of wary look.

'I neither like nor dislike him,' he said. 'He is . . . simply there. Obviously my mother chose him as her partner and I have to respect that. I suppose I must get on with it the best I can.'

This seemed, to William, a decidedly evasive reply. 'You must have an opinion of him,' he prompted.

'Must I?' asked Toby, who seemed not to like this line of enquiry. 'I'll tell you this: Seth Jessop is the sort of fellow who always gets his way in the end. I wouldn't want to be the one to go against him.'

'Against him in what?' asked William.

'In anything,' said Toby. 'Seen enough here?' he asked, and when William nodded he led them on towards the quarry itself, pointing out various structures along the way and explaining how in his grandfather's day the slates had been carried to the port by packhorses. Since the installation of the rail track, productivity had increased considerably and Jessop Quarry had an advantage over many of the others in the area. But apparently this wasn't enough for Seth. 'He's been talking about putting in steam engines,' said Toby. 'That way we wouldn't have to use horses to tow the wagons back uphill from the dock. Seth wants us to be the first quarry in Wales to have steam.'

'Do you suppose that will happen?'

Toby smiled. 'It's like I said. If Seth decides he wants something, it happens, one way or another.'

Now they were descending the long ramp that led down to the floor of the quarry. Gazing up at the high walls ahead and on either side of him, William was able to fully appreciate the massive scale of them. He gazed up at the figures of the men working the gallery and marvelled at their agility, noting that each man had a length of rope tied off around one thigh and was using this to move across the rock face, looking for openings in which to insert the long metal crowbar he carried. Whenever they found a suitable place, they would slip the bar in and exert pressure. When it became apparent that something was about to give, the man would yell a warning and swing nimbly out of harm's way; and a huge block of slate would begin to fall.

'Sometimes they use black blasting powder to knock down the bigger pieces,' said Toby. '*Powdwr du*, they call it. That's always worth seeing, but they don't seem to be using any at the moment.'

Toby and William moved slowly nearer, picking their way across the jumble of slates that littered the floor. A workman, noticing Toby's unsuitable clothing, called out a warning. 'Probably best not to get any closer, young sir,' he warned. 'It can be dangerous.'

Toby gave him a contemptuous look. 'I know what I'm doing,' he snapped, and the man bowed his head apologetically. But William couldn't help thinking that the advice had been sound enough. The men working at floor level knew exactly how to get out of harm's way when something was about to fall, but Toby, bundled up in his heavy overcoat, wouldn't be anything like as nimble.

'Perhaps that really is close enough,' suggested William.

But Toby seemed caught up in his own thoughts, musing aloud about the future of slate mining. 'They say this is the fastest-growing industry in Wales,' he told William, moving closer. 'When your grandfather had this place, he was making perhaps five or ten thousand pounds profit a year.'

'Gosh!'

'I know that might sound a lot, but Seth told me just the other day that he expects the quarry will make a *hundred* thousand pounds profit this year.' He turned to look at William, smiling at the very thought of it. 'Imagine that, William – a hundred thousand pounds! All from this stuff.' He bent over and picked up a little piece of slate, and in that same instant a movement high above them caught William's eye. He glanced up in surprise to see that a big expanse of grey, up at the top edge of the gallery, was beginning to shift. Nobody appeared to have prised it free, so there was nobody to shout a warning...

Toby straightened up, holding out the shard of slate for William to look at. 'It's just mud, you know. Mud from millions of years ago, compressed by the weight of tons of rock lying on top if it. Seth says...'

But William wasn't listening. He was gazing up in horrified fascination as the massive grey block slid suddenly forward, hit a protrusion and then tilted forward, turning lazily in the air. Then it was hurtling downwards, end over end, straight towards Toby.

For a moment William almost went with his instincts and ran, but somehow he caught himself and threw himself straight at Toby. He wrapped his arms around the boy, knocking him clean off his feet and sending the two of them down in an ungainly sprawl onto the litter of broken slates beneath them. Toby opened his mouth to protest, but in that same instant a shadow fell across them as the falling block hurtled past and hit the ground in a shower of dust just inches from their outstretched feet, the impact seeming to shake the very earth beneath them, turning the smaller stones beneath it into flying shards of gravel. The block rolled over once, twice and then lay still. Dust rolled in to obliterate everything, making William cough violently and then, almost instantly, it began to clear.

William stared at the place where the block had first struck the ground and he noticed a tattered piece of shiny black material lying flat on the uneven surface. It took him a few moments to recognise it for what it was – all that was left of Toby's top hat. Beyond the fallen rock, a straggle of men stood, staring open-mouthed at the fallen boys; and then, a moment later, realising what had just happened, they burst into spontaneous applause.

William got unsteadily to his feet and was instantly surrounded by the workmen, who were patting him on the back, telling him he'd done an amazing thing. Toby just lay there, his face frozen in an expression of shock as it began to dawn on him how close he'd come to dying.

Just then a familiar figure appeared, pushing his way through the crowd of men, and stood there looking down at Toby.

'What in God's name happened here?' snapped Seth curtly.

'Sir, they got too close,' said a workman, but Seth dismissed him with a wave of his hand. He stared down at Toby.

'Well, boy?' he snarled.

Toby finally found his voice. 'Sir...a big slab fell. I do believe...William just saved my life.' He pointed to the tattered remains of the hat.

Seth continued to stare at Toby. For a moment an expression flitted across his thin face, one that shocked William, because, just for an instant, it looked almost like one of disappointment. Seth glanced up at the gallery, and

William followed his gaze, just in time to see somebody ducking back out of sight into a hollow near the top of the quarry. William thought that he saw the briefest flash of red. He looked at Seth again, but the expression was gone now, replaced by the usual hostile glare. William waited for Seth to say something, but he didn't. Instead he reached down and helped Toby back to his feet, then brushed some slate dust from his coat with his free hand.

'Come,' he said at last. 'My business here is concluded. We'll head back to the Rise.' And he turned and made his way across the quarry, as though the matter was dismissed. William and Toby exchanged puzzled looks, then followed him in silence.

CHAPTER TWELVE
THE MIST

As the growler headed back uphill, another mist began to fall. By the time they had reached the deserted streets of Porthmadog it was hard to see more than a few feet in front of them, but the horses seemed to know their way and kept up a steady trot, their hooves echoing on the cobbled road. The occasional cloaked figure drifted past them on the streets.

William sat beside Idris again, wondering what to make of the latest developments. He had just saved Toby's life, something that should surely have deserved a mention, a brief thank-you, *something*. But Seth had climbed back inside the coach without so much as a word, and Toby had got meekly in beside him and that, it seemed, was to be the end of the matter. William found himself wondering about the 'accident'. Was it just William's imagination, or had Seth really looked disappointed by the outcome? Had he been looking up at the gallery to locate somebody who was hidden up there? An accomplice? Was that why he had encouraged William to go to the quarry in the first place? Because he wanted to be rid of him? He remembered how Seth had insisted that Toby show William the gallery. 'Get in close,' he'd said. And then he'd taunted Toby, saying he was scared.

William told himself his mind was working overtime. Why would Seth want to do something like that? William was working for nothing, wasn't he? He was making himself useful around the house. And besides, Toby had been standing right there with him and the boulder that had fallen had been big enough to kill both of them. Surely... surely Seth wouldn't have risked killing his stepson as well? But then William thought about the disparaging looks that Seth threw at Toby whenever they were together. As though he actually disliked the boy. As though he actually *hated* him. And with Toby out of the way, William thought, Seth would keep his hold on Jessop Quarry *and* the Ransome estate. He would be wealthier than ever.

Then William found himself thinking about what Idris had told him... something that had sounded very unlike Seth... that business about him crying over the contents of a box.

He leaned closer to Idris, not wanting to be overheard by the passengers. 'Idris,' he whispered, 'you know what you told me yesterday? About seeing my uncle in the old chapel?'

'What about it?' asked Idris, much too loudly, and William had to lift a finger to his lips.

'Shush! Do you . . . do you think you could show me the place, some time?'

Idris had got the message and couched the rest of his replies in an exaggerated stage whisper. 'Idris can show you. When do we go?'

William frowned. 'That's the problem. I can't let anyone else know I'm going there. They'd only ask questions.' He thought for a moment. 'Mrs Craddock calls me at six o'clock, every morning,' he said. 'Do you think we could go there and be back *before* six?'

Idris looked confused, and William remembered that he didn't really understand numbers, so he rephrased the question. 'If I come to the stable very early, before the sun comes up, could you take me there and then bring me straight back again, before it gets light?'

Idris nodded. 'Oh yes. Idris can do that. We can ride Maggie.'

'Oh, I . . . I can't ride,' hissed William.

'Do not worry. Idris will show you. Easy it is. Very easy. And too far to walk and get back quick.'

'Well, all right then. Tomorrow morning?'

'Tomorrow, yes! Idris will be ready.' He looked thoughtful. 'Mr Jessop rode out on Sabre last night,' he said. 'He came to the stable after dinner.'

'Where did he go?' asked William.

'I think to Porthmadog. He smelled of wine when he came back.'

'Perhaps he went to the chapel again?'

'No. He took the other road. Came back very late.'

William wondered about that. Had Seth gone to Porthmadog to talk to an accomplice? To set up today's 'accident'? Or was William's imagination running away with him?

The coach was heading through the outskirts of Porthmadog now and beginning the long slow climb up to the clifftop.

'Didn't you think to have a look?' whispered William. 'When you saw him at the chapel that time? Didn't you want to see what was in that box?'

Idris frowned, shook his head. 'Some things Idris doesn't want to know,' he said mysteriously. 'Some things *you* don't want to know, neither.'

William wondered if Idris had a point. Would he regret going to look? But something about it was too powerful to resist. He needed to know what it was that could make an implacable man like Seth Jessop break down in tears. It had to be something important.

They were heading up the steep incline to the clifftop now, the horses straining to keep the coach moving. Up here, the mist was thicker and William could only just make out the craggy outlines of the rocks that fringed either side of the road. They looked like dragon's teeth, he thought, or at least what he imagined such things might look like. When he detected a movement to his left, he snapped his gaze in that direction and thought he caught a glimpse of a cloaked figure, amidst the rocks, moving alongside the coach with a strange gliding motion, as though the uneven track and poor visibility were no obstacles. 'What's that?' he asked, pointing, but the moment he spoke, he could see nothing but the jagged shapes of the stone.

'What's what?' asked Idris, mystified.

'Oh, it's just that I thought I...' He broke off as he became aware of another movement, this time on the opposite side of the road. He leaned forward to see past Idris, but once again the tall moving figure he thought he had glimpsed seemed to have disappeared. He told himself that he must be imagining things; nobody was fast enough to cross the road in such a short space of time, and it was hardly likely that there was more than one person out on this desolate track in such weather. He forced himself to look away, but his bemusement must have been obvious.

'What's wrong, Will'yam? asked Idris. 'You look worried.'

'It's probably nothing. I thought I saw...' He broke off again, because now he could see, quite clearly, another figure, sitting cross-legged on a high rock, up on the left-hand side of the road, gazing down at the coach, its hooded face hidden from view. The figure was lit by an unearthly yellow glow. As the coach drew nearer, the figure stayed reassuringly solid. William pointed.

'Look there, Idris,' he said. 'You can see that, can't you?'

Idris stared for a moment and then smiled. 'Oh aye,' he said.

'You...you *can*?' William prompted him, not understanding why Idris was so calm about it. 'Really?'

Idris nodded, grinned. He pulled the coach to a halt and gazed up at the figure, which, as William stared in abject terror, got slowly to its feet and began to climb down the rocks to the road. Now William could see that the eerie light was coming from a lantern, which the figure carried in one hand.

'Why have we stopped?' growled Seth's voice from inside the coach.

But William couldn't reply – because now the figure was drifting across the road, the lantern held out in front of it. It was standing right beside the coach. It was clambering up onto the bench seat...

'Move over a bit,' said Rhiannon.

William let out a long sigh of relief. 'What are *you* doing here?' he gasped.

'Mrs Craddock was worried you might need a light in this fog. She sent me out to wait for you.' She looked sharply at William. 'Are you going to move over?'

'Oh yes, of course.' He slid sideways to make space for her to sit down.

'It's bad, this,' observed Rhiannon. 'It's like Mrs Craddock's porridge,' she added, gazing around. 'Thick ...'

'... and salty,' muttered William. She gave him an odd look. Idris flicked the reins and the horses started on their way again, making the coach lurch forward. 'How did you cross the road so quickly?' William asked her.

She gave him a baffled look. 'What are you on about?' she asked him.

'I saw you moving before,' he explained. 'On *that* side –'

he pointed – 'and then on that side.'

'I don't think you did,' she told him. 'I've been waiting there for ages.'

'You . . . you didn't cross the road?'

'No. Why would I?'

'But I thought—'

He broke off as a long screeching noise came from somewhere behind them. Rhiannon glanced back over her shoulder. 'What was that?' she asked.

'An owl?' said Idris.

'That didn't sound like an owl,' said Rhiannon fearfully. 'It sounded more like the *Gwrach*!'

'Oh, don't start on about that again,' said William. 'I'm sure it was just—' But the sound came again, long, mournful and surely louder than any owl had the right to be, seeming to echo in the mist. Just then Seth leaned his head out of the window, his thin face paler than usual.

'Can't you get this thing moving any faster?' he snapped.

'Oh, sir,' said Idris, 'it's not safe to go fast in this fog. I can't see—'

'Do it!' growled Seth. 'Now.'

'Yes, sir.' Idris hunched forward and slapped the reins down hard. 'Giddy-up!' he said, and the horses lunged forward, jolting the coach and its occupants. William clung on tightly. It seemed like madness to go faster, for he could hardly see ten feet ahead of them. The screeching sound came again, shrill and sustained. Rhiannon glanced back over her shoulder and said, 'I think there's something following us!'

'Nonsense,' said William, but he wished he could feel as confident as he sounded. As the coach accelerated along the rough road, the wooden seat began to jounce and sway, threatening to throw him off, but despite that he found himself compelled to stand upright, twisting around so he could look back over the shuddering roof of the carriage. The fog was now so thick he could only see a short distance, but it seemed to him that there *was* something moving in the mist, just above the surface of the road, something that writhed and flapped as it flew through the air in pursuit. It didn't look like an owl. It didn't look like anything that he'd ever seen before.

Seth was leaning out of the window again. 'Faster!' he roared, and, glancing down at him, William was shocked to see something in his uncle's face that he'd never seen there before. Fear: sheer terror.

'Sir,' pleaded Idris, 'we could break an axle!'

'I'll break your neck if you don't get this carriage moving,' Seth promised him, and Idris had no option but to comply. He snorted at the horses and they reacted as readily as if he'd laid a whip across their backs. The carriage gave another lurch and Rhiannon, struggling to hold on, dropped the lantern. It fell to the road beside them and smashed, erupting in a sudden burst of flame, and as the fire was left behind William finally got a clearer view of what was following the coach.

It was a woman, he decided, or at least it had been once. Now it was a wizened thing, a nightmare of twisted limbs and exposed bone; what was keeping it soaring above the road was a pair of leathery wings, like those of a huge bat, extending out on either side of the creature's shrouded body. As it passed over the flame, William saw its face; the staring eyes, the haggard wasted cheeks, the black teeth and a hideous lolling tongue of the same midnight hue.

He glimpsed it for only an instant, and then the flame was left behind and the fog closed in again. William could no longer be sure if the thing was still following them, but suddenly Rhiannon's tales of the *Gwrach y Rhibyn* – the Hag of the Mist – no longer seemed quite so fanciful.

'Is there something behind us?' he heard Rhiannon cry. He looked down at her and saw that her gaze was still fixed on the way ahead, as though she was afraid to look for herself.

'I . . . I'm not sure,' he told her.

With a last effort the horses made it over the final rise to where the road levelled out. Ahead of them, through the fog, they could see the looming ghostly outline of Jessop Rise standing on the clifftop. Idris allowed the horses to slow as they approached the gates, and a few moments later he was pulling up at the front of the house. No sooner had the coach come to a halt than the door flew open and Seth leaped out. He ran to the front door of the house and began to pound on it with a gloved fist. After a few moments it was opened by a startled-looking Mrs Craddock. Seth pushed her roughly aside and disappeared within. She looked after him for a moment and then turned back – Toby was peering out through the open door of the coach, and the other three were still arranged on the wooden seat, staring down at her in bemusement.

'What was the big hurry?' asked Mrs Craddock, but if anybody knew the answer to that, they weren't ready to tell her.

CHAPTER THIRTEEN
THE CHAPEL

After the strangeness of the frantic chase from the quarry, things seemed to slip back to their usual pattern. Rhiannon and Mrs Craddock set to work in the kitchen and William went about his tasks around the house. After some consideration he decided not to tell Rhiannon what he had seen on the road back from the quarry in the vivid blaze of her dropped lantern. The girl was nervous enough without having her worst nightmares confirmed. And as the hours passed, William had to ask himself if he really *had* seen what he thought he had. Was it not just some kind of turbulence in the mist – an illusion conjured from that sudden burst of flame?

At the time he had been convinced that he was actually looking at the *Gwrach y Rhibyn*. Now he didn't feel quite so sure.

That night he waited at table, while Seth and Toby ate

their meal in silence. But after they had finished dining, Seth looked up at William and smiled thinly at him.

'Regarding your quick actions at the quarry today,' he said, 'Toby wanted to express his gratitude and has asked me to reward you.' And he reached into his waistcoat pocket and pulled out a coin, a gold sovereign, which he attempted to push into William's hand.

William shook his head. 'There's no need for that,' he assured Seth. 'I only did what anyone would have done.'

This seemed to amuse Seth. 'You hear that, Toby?' he said. 'It would seem your cousin is a nobler sort than you.'

Toby looked up from his plate in surprise. 'Why do you say that?'

'I have no doubt that in similar circumstances, you'd have taken the money without hesitation.'

Toby scowled. 'I'm sorry to be such a disappointment to you,' he said. He glared at his stepfather. 'Why must you constantly remind me how much I fail to measure up to your expectations?' He transferred his attention to William. 'Take the coin,' he muttered. 'It's worth twenty shillings. You could buy yourself something with it. A decent coat . . . some boots.'

'It's very kind,' said William, 'but I didn't help you because I wanted a reward. I did it because you are my cousin and I wanted to protect you.'

This seemed to shock Toby. He sat there looking at William, open-mouthed, and then without another word he jumped up from his seat and left the room. William started to go after him, but Seth reined him in.

'Let him stew,' he said. 'You have shamed him, that's all.'

'I didn't mean to,' William assured him.

'I'm sure you didn't. But you have done so anyway.' He slapped the coin down on the table. 'By God, but you remind me of your father!' he snapped. 'Why won't you take the money?'

'I cannot,' said William. 'Not for doing something that any decent person would have done.'

Seth considered his words for a moment. 'Very well,' he said. 'Let's call it a payment. For all the work you've done around the house since you came. How would that be?'

'Better,' said William. 'And something I feel I *have* earned.' He picked up the coin and slipped it in his pocket. 'Thank you, uncle.'

Seth chuckled. 'Just don't go making the mistake of thinking it will be a regular occurrence. It's a one-off payment for services rendered.' He shook his head, smiled. 'It's true you have more spirit than Toby,' he observed. 'That boy is a mystery to me. He seems to have no ambition whatsoever...no interest in the advantages that his inheritance can give him. In different circumstances I've no doubt at all that you'd make a better heir than he. But you are Matthew's boy and, sadly for you, that means you shall never advance any further in life.' He got to his feet. 'Your father denied you everything. Just remember that.'

With that he got to his feet and swaggered out of the room, leaving William to clear the table.

William was on the beach, digging for all he was worth, the spade in his blistered hands delving deeper and deeper into the clinging wet sand. It was night-time and he was crouched beside a row of black rocks. When he paused to glance up, he could see the full moon riding on a sea of clouds, its yellow reflection glinting off the restless ocean. Black shapes flapped above the water. Crows. But what were they doing here on the beach? Shouldn't they be gulls? The wind wailed and moaned like a thing alive. He wasn't sure what had brought him out here so late; he only knew that something lay beneath the sand, waiting for the sharp edge of his spade to strike it...so he kept digging, and as he worked, he sensed that somewhere close by unseen eyes were watching him, waiting impatiently for him to find whatever was buried down there...

He woke suddenly and lay in the darkness of his room, terrified, his heart thudding in his chest, because he was convinced that a cold hand had just stroked his cheek. He lay on his back, trying to rein in his mounting panic, and he had a sudden, all-pervading feeling that he had forgotten something really important...but what? Then it came to him in a rush. Yes, of course! He was supposed to be meeting Idris this morning! He had promised to be at the stable well before dawn. He'd tried to stay awake through the long night because he had no way of waking himself up at a particular hour, but tiredness had eventually overwhelmed him and, though he'd tried to fight it off, slumber had finally claimed him. Then he'd started dreaming about the beach again...

There was a soft creaking sound as the door to his room swung slowly open, admitting some light. He turned to look, dreading the sight of Mrs Craddock standing in the doorway, roused once again by the noises he'd been making in his sleep, but there was nobody there, just an upright oblong of paler darkness, and that was somehow infinitely more worrying. He reached out to the candle and matches and thankfully, for once, they were exactly where he'd left them. His trembling hands managed to get the candle alight and he looked anxiously around the room, but there was nobody else there. Who then had touched his face? Had it been part of the dream? And just as troubling, who had opened the door? He crept out of bed, found his clothes and pulled them on, although he did not know what time it was. He decided to leave his boots until he was downstairs, so he tied the laces together and hung them around his neck. Then, taking up the candle, he went carefully out of the room, desperate to avoid waking Mrs Craddock.

Closing the door gently behind him, he stood listening on the landing for a moment and soon heard a deep, rhythmic snoring coming from Mrs Craddock's room. He crept down the first flight of stairs, placing his feet with care. On the second-floor landing, a grandfather clock informed him that it was a little after 4 a.m., exactly the time he had intended heading out to the stable. He thought again about the hand that had touched his face. Had it been done to wake him at just the right time? But he didn't want to think too much about that. The idea that he had a ghostly guardian, making sure that he kept his appointments, was an unsettling idea.

He made it down to the ground floor and stood for a moment, hardly daring to breathe, terrified of waking the dogs, who slept in the dining room, in front of the dying embers of the fire. But there was no sound from that direction. He crept to the scullery where he put on his boots. Then, as quietly as he could, he drew back the heavy bolts on the back door and swung it open, only to find that the fog had worsened in the night and he could now see barely more than two steps in front of him. For an instant, part of him recoiled. He told himself that he should abandon this madness and make his way back up to his still-warm bed, but he had come this far and he decided that it would be silly to turn back now. Besides, Idris would be expecting him. So he blew out the candle and stepped quickly outside, pulling the door gently shut behind him.

The cold hit him then, an awful chill that seemed to worm itself into his bones. He shrugged the roomy coat tighter around himself and set off along the path, his arms crossed in front of him, his breath clouding around his head like a frozen halo. He kept walking until the stables block finally loomed out of the greyness, big and foreboding, and he saw that the main door was slightly ajar.

'Idris?' he whispered. 'Idris, are you awake?'

No answer. He took a couple of steps further into the silence of the stable, peering up to the open entrance of the hayloft.

'Idris? It's me, W—'

A hand settled on his shoulder with such unexpectedness he nearly jumped out of his skin. He spun around with a gasp of fear, only to see Idris's grinning face a few inches from his own.

'H'lo, Will'yam,'

'Idris! You ... you scared me.'

Idris put his head to one side and looked puzzled at this. 'But ... it is only Idris,' he said. 'No need to be scared.'

'Yes, I know that now.' William tried to shrug off his fear. 'Are you ... are you ready to go?'

Idris nodded. 'All ready,' he said brightly. 'Idris has been waiting.' He walked over to Maggie's stall, slipped inside and then led her out. William saw that the roan horse was already fitted with a bridle and a leather saddle. A pair of canvas saddle bags were draped across her withers. Idris handed the reins to William who took them uncertainly and hurried across to push the exterior doors wider. He peered outside, sniffing the air. 'Foggy,' he said. 'Cold.'

'Yes. Will that be a problem?'

Idris shook his shaggy head. 'Maggie knows the way,' he said, matter-of-factly. He came back and in one lithe movement vaulted nimbly up into the saddle. Then he reached down a hand to William.

'I've never ridden before,' William reminded him.

'No matter,' said Idris. He took William's hand in his and, displaying incredible strength for one so scrawny, pulled him up and around behind him. 'Now hang on tight,' he said. 'We take short cut.' He clicked his tongue and Maggie started forward. In moments they were out of the barn and trotting across the grass, around the side of the house, which William was only dimly aware of, a great brooding shape off to his left. Once past the building, Idris made a gentle snorting sound and Maggie picked up the pace, heading towards the entrance gate. It loomed suddenly out of the mist, looking for all the world like the open jaws of a huge beast advancing out of the fog.

Once they were through the gate and onto the clifftop beyond, Idris drummed his heels into Maggie's flanks and urged her into a gallop. William hung on tight around Idris's waist and peered over his shoulder, wishing he could see something. It felt distinctly odd. There was the sense of frantic motion beneath him, the thudding of hooves against the frozen ground, but aside from the glimpsed shape of an occasional tree or shrub drifting past them, he had no idea where he was or where they were headed. He could hear the sound of the ocean away to his right and there was the sharp, salt smell of it on the frozen air, but for all he knew they could be riding across the sky, Maggie's hooves drumming against nothing more substantial than clouds.

He did not know how long they rode in this fashion. Tired as he was, and lulled by Maggie's relentless rhythm, William's mind began to drift. Sleep clawed at the edges of his consciousness and he sank into a half-slumber, images flickering through his unconscious mind like magic-lantern slides – images of the beach where he'd been digging in his dream, the sharp spade cleaving the damp sand aside – so when Maggie snorted and pulled suddenly to a halt, it came as something of a surprise.

'What's wrong?' he gasped.

'Maggie does not like this place,' said Idris, pointing to a faint outline in the mist. William stared and realised that it was the circle of standing stones, the ones he had seen in the distance the night he arrived. Maggie did indeed seem to be agitated. She was shaking her head, kicking her feet.

'What's wrong with her?' whispered William.

'This place is very old,' said Idris. 'People used to pray here, before they had churches. Maggie can smell the wrongness of it.'

'Isn't it . . . where the *Gwrach* is supposed to live?' he murmured.

Idris nodded. He clicked his tongue and Maggie started slowly forward, but she was still skittish. As they moved past the circle William turned to look back over his shoulder and it seemed to him that something *was* moving at the very heart of the structure – something that flapped and swirled rhythmically within the drifting banks of mist. Then there was a sudden screech and a whole flock of dark shapes burst up from ground level and careered off in all directions.

Crows, William told himself, relieved, but it didn't stop his heart from hammering in his chest. As though galvanised by the appearance of the birds, Maggie took off into another gallop and they continued on their way across the frozen ground.

'Not too far now,' said Idris. William nodded and tried to stay alert but soon began to drift off again. More images of the moonlit beach spilled through his head and then he was digging once more, the spade cutting deeper, deeper into the wet sand...

And then, once again, Maggie slowed to a walk.

'We're here,' announced Idris.

William blinked the sleep from his eyes. Glancing around, he saw that they were just emerging from a stand of trees. They came to a place where the ground dropped steeply away, and William peered intently into the darkness. After a few moments he managed to discern the shape of a ruined building in an open space some distance below them. Idris walked Maggie a little closer and indicated where a narrow footpath led down to the clearing. The shape of the building became steadily more visible – a grey stone chapel, the roof long gone, gaunt broken beams stabbing at the heavens. Most of one long wall had fallen down too and its stones were scattered across the ground.

'I watch Mr Jessop from up here,' said Idris quietly. 'From the trees. Idris can see right inside the chapel.' Again he pulled Maggie to a halt. He reached back, slipped an arm around William's waist and swung him to the ground. Then he unbuckled one of the sacks behind him and pulled out a greasy-looking oil lamp, which he handed down to William.

'There,' he said. 'Now you can light your way.'

'Aren't you coming with me?' asked William anxiously.

Idris shook his head. 'I wait here,' he said, handing William a box of matches. 'With Maggie.' He watched as William lowered the lamp to the ground and then struggled to get the thing alight, his fingers nearly numb with the cold. As the wick finally lit, William saw in the sudden glow that Idris's feet in the stirrups were completely bare and he wondered how the man could endure such a thing. His feet must be beyond frozen.

William stood up and lifted the lamp. He gazed imploringly at Idris. 'Are you sure you won't come along?' he said.

Idris nodded. 'Idris not like such places,' he said. 'I wait here.'

William nodded, realising that this was not the time to argue. He needed to deal with this and get back to the house before his absence was noticed. So he turned towards the steep path and descended it carefully, not wanting to trip and extinguish his only source of light. Once he was level with the building, he had a better view of it. The ancient wooden door stood open, much of it rotted away. A crudely made metal cross was affixed to the wall above the door.

It was red with rust, long trails marking the stone like trickles of dark blood.

William went inside and stood looking at the shadowy, ruined interior of the chapel. The remains of rows of wooden pews stood on either side of a narrow central aisle, but anything of value must have been stripped out of the place years ago. The stone flags were littered with dead leaves and broken twigs and the two stained-glass windows on the intact wall to his left had been shattered. Up at the top end of the room, the oblong platform of the large altar awaited him. Idris had told him that what he was seeking was hidden under the altar and he wished now he'd asked for more details. But he lifted the lantern higher and started walking along the aisle, his feet rustling the frozen leaves.

As he walked, he got the distinct feeling that he wasn't alone here; so much so that he stopped halfway and looked around at the broken pews on either side of him, but as far as he could tell the place was deserted. He continued walking until finally he reached the altar, which was just a simple stone block, about as high as a man's waist. He held the lantern close to examine it, but the front-facing part at least was solid and showed no place where something might be hidden. He moved around to the far side and there *was* a recess under the back of it, an opening through which he could see the raised wooden rostrum on which the altar stood. He knelt down and moved the lantern into the recess. Now he saw that several of the ancient wooden boards had been carefully sawn through, a foot or so apart, and that a metal clasp had been sunk into the centre of one of them. William took it between thumb and forefinger and gave a sharp tug. The board lifted away, revealing an opening beneath.

William stood the lantern to the side and leaned down to try to see what might be in there, but it was no use. The light wouldn't reach to that depth and he realised, with a shiver of apprehension, that he was going to have to reach into the darkness and feel around, a prospect that filled him with dread. Who knew what might be hidden in there? Nevertheless, he steeled himself and slid his right hand in through the opening, steeling himself to touch whatever his outstretched fingers encountered. Visions danced in his head – slugs, rats, spiders – but he shrugged them off and sank his arm in to the elbow. After a few moments his fingers found something hard and unyielding – what felt like the edge of a wooden box. William explored it with his fingertips and found a cold metal handle. He managed to get a grip on this with his forefinger and thumb and he pulled...

The end of a large wooden casket slid into view; a handsome thing made of polished oak and decorated with metal embellishments. He felt a brief thrill of exhilaration. It was here! He had found the thing that had so preoccupied Seth! With a little effort he managed to tilt the casket to a forty-five-degree angle and then pulled it up through the opening. It wasn't particularly heavy and he set it down on the floor beside the altar, his excitement rising.

He went to lift the lid and felt a pulse of disappointment when he realised that the box was locked. He rocked back on his knees, wondering what to do now. If he broke the casket open, then Seth would know that somebody had been snooping here – but at the same time he couldn't just walk away; he had to know what was inside. He thought for a moment and then an idea occurred to him. He moved back to the opening and reached into the hole once again, this time fearless about what might be in there. A notion had come to him that perhaps the key was hidden in there too. He reached down and his fingers touched a hard earth floor. He moved his hand from side to side, questing, searching, but finding nothing. Eventually he decided he was wasting his time. He was about to draw his hand out again when a noise made him flinch – a sudden metallic clank, from somewhere above him, the unmistakable sound of metal falling onto stone.

He pulled his hand free and snatched up the lantern. He started to get to his feet, but froze mid-crouch when his head came level with the top of the altar and he noticed that something was lying on top of it – a large, metal key. He snatched in a breath and stared at the object, knowing full well that it hadn't been there a moment ago; he would have sworn to the fact. He looked frantically around the church, but once again, as far as he could tell, he was alone. Reaching out with his free hand he picked up the key. It was icy cold to the touch.

William sank slowly down again, asking himself what kind of madness was happening here. How could a key suddenly appear out of thin air? And who – or what – was helping him in his search? And why? Taking a deep breath, he set the lantern down on the floor again and, with a trembling hand, he slotted the key into the lock. It fitted perfectly. Of course it did. He exerted a little pressure and the lock clicked open.

He looked at the box for a moment and licked his lips. Part of him was reluctant to open it, realising that if he did, he would have gone too far to turn back. Perhaps Idris had been right when he said it was better not to know some things. And yet... William needed to know. He *had* to know.

He reached out again and gripped the decorative edge of the lid. 'It's just a box,' he whispered to himself. 'There's no reason to be scared. No reason at all.' Then he lifted the lid and stared at what lay inside.

A scream filled the chapel, a scream that seemed to echo on the night air, high and shrill like the cry of a child. William knelt there frozen, struggling to regain his breath. It was several moments before the truth dawned on him. The scream had come from him.

CHAPTER FOURTEEN
THE CASKET

It lay on a purple cushion, grinning up at him. William saw it and knew instantly what it was, but couldn't help wondering why it was so *small*. He leaned back from the box and allowed his breathing to return to normal.

It was the remains of a body, and to be such a size, he told himself, it must be that of a baby. Sure enough, beside the lace pillow on which the shrivelled head was resting lay a pretty rattle, decorated with what looked like pearls. The baby's body was mostly bone now, what remained of the flesh grey and shrunken. William felt tears welling in his eyes. Death was something to which he was well used, there had already been enough of it in his young life to harden him to the reality of it, but this was all that was left of a young child, a creature who had barely had time to experience anything of the world. Why was Seth keeping it out here in this secret place? Why had it not been given a proper Christian burial?

William's thoughts were interrupted by a low moaning sound and he felt a chill settle on him that was nothing to do with the cold. There was somebody else here. Filled with dread, he knelt up again and peered fearfully over the top of the altar. To his horror, he saw that there was now a figure sitting in one of the pews to his left. It was the woman from the clifftop path, shrouded in her hooded cloak. She was sitting hunched in her seat, one white hand resting on the back of the pew in front of her. Her shoulders were moving up and down, and as William gazed, rooted to the spot in terror, he realised that the sound he had heard was of her sobbing.

'Who are you?' he whispered, but the woman didn't answer. She seemed completely caught up in her own anguish, her head bowed, her shoulders shaking with some unspeakable sorrow.

William turned his attention back to the casket. He had seen its contents now and there seemed little point in dwelling on them, so he closed the lid, turned the key in the lock and then pulled it free. Reaching up, he set the key back on top of the altar and returned the casket to its dark hiding place, sliding it along the earth floor until it was out of sight. Then, with shaking hands, he put the wooden cover back into position and started to get to his feet.

That was his first intimation that the woman had moved. As he straightened up, she was leaning on the altar, staring directly into his eyes, her face inches from his. As ever, her features were lost in the terrible darkness of that hood, but he could feel once again the intensity of her gaze burning into his very soul.

'Bring him to me!' she croaked, the voice seeming to blast into his face like a cold wind gusting in off the ocean, bringing with it a heady odour of lavender. The same perfume he had noticed in Mistress Audrina's room at Jessop Rise.

He reeled back, lifting an arm to cover his face, steeling himself to make a run for it, but when he took the arm away again he was relieved to discover that she was gone and he was once more alone in the chapel. He glanced down at the altar and saw that the key too had vanished.

He didn't linger. He grabbed up the lantern and made for the door at a brisk pace. He had seen everything he needed to. Now he wanted to be out of here and back in the relative warmth and security of Jessop Rise. At the entrance he paused for a moment to look warily outside. The fog was still thick, but he could see the beginning of the track, leading up the steep incline where he hoped and prayed that Idris would still be waiting for him.

Halfway up, something made him pause and glance back. He could just make out the outline of the chapel's ruined doorway, and now he was once again aware of a figure, standing beside it, watching him intently. She was wrapped up in her grey cloak and was once again holding her lantern, but the glow of it was faint, still not powerful enough to illuminate her features. William tried to order his thoughts, because it seemed to him that the creature he thought he had seen following the growler through the fog the other day hadn't been this woman, but something else entirely. Could there really be two ghostly apparitions haunting the house? Before he left Northwich he had not believed in the existence of such things, and if asked would have declared the subject utter nonsense, but since his arrival here his beliefs had been rocked to their very core. Now he no longer knew what to believe.

He turned away and hurried on up to the top of the slope. He heard the soft snort of a horse ahead of him, a few steps before the outline of Maggie loomed out of the fog. Idris was slumped in the saddle, seemingly dozing.

'Hey!' hissed William, and Idris jerked awake, looking startled. He gazed down at William.

'It was there?' he asked. 'The hidden thing?'

William nodded, and Idris reached down a hand to take the lantern from him. He blew out the flame, then reached back to tie the lantern to his saddlebag.

'You were gone a long time,' said Idris.

William nodded grimly. 'I saw something else in there,' he said. 'Something bad.'

Idris scowled, then reached down a hand to help William back into the saddle. Idris clucked his tongue and Maggie started walking back towards the trees.

'Well, don't you want to know what it was?' asked William.

Idris shook his head. 'Best Idris doesn't know,' he said. He spurred Maggie forward into a trot, a canter and then a gallop.

'You really don't care?' William yelled into his ear as they raced along the woodland track.

Again a dismissive shake of the head. It was clear that Idris preferred to remain in ignorance. He urged Maggie headlong into the mist, and once again William had that weird feeling of falling into a rhythm, without actually going anywhere. He clung on, wondering how Maggie knew where she was headed. Perhaps she didn't, he thought glumly, and at any moment she might plunge over a cliff, taking herself and her two riders to destruction. And serve them right for venturing out on a morning as hostile as this one.

Images seethed and roiled in William's head. He couldn't stop himself from picturing the two ghostly women, one intent on watching the house, the other hardly human at all but a hideous shrivelled creature that had followed the coach like some predatory bird, flapping her great wings. And then he thought about what he had found hidden in the casket just now, the grinning grey face that had gazed so intently up at him as if challenging him to guess at its origins. William tried to make himself think practically about it. Why would the remains of a baby be kept there in that remote place? Why would it not have had a proper Christian burial?

And, William asked himself, why would Seth go to that ruined chapel to look at those tragic remains? Could it be the child was his? The woman weeping in the chapel pew, was that Audrina? The lavender smell? The eerie goings-on in her room? Was she trying to tell him something? Was it *her* child hidden in the casket? And if so, did it have anything to do with her disappearance?

Something cold spattered his face, sending icy needles through his already chilled features. He lifted his head slightly to peer over Idris's shoulder and realised that it had started to snow, the frozen drops slanting down through the air, driven by the rising wind. Above him the sky seemed to be gradually lightening. It wasn't long before morning and he had no idea how far they still had to go.

Then he became aware of something away to his right: the circle of stones they had passed on the way here. He could see them a little better now, looking strangely spectral in the half-light. Maggie was snorting and tossing her head again, as though scared, and then William saw a possible reason for that. Standing in the centre of the circle was the cloaked woman with her lantern. She was beckoning to William, as though inviting him to join her in the circle. But it didn't seem an inviting prospect. He tapped Idris on the shoulder. 'Can you see that?' he asked, pointing to the woman.

'The circle?' asked Idris. 'You saw that before.'

'No, *inside* the circle. Can you see a woman?'

'No,' said Idris, but he wasn't even looking in that direction. He urged Maggie onwards, until they had left the stones far behind.

'Well, you could at least have looked!'

Idris shook his head and kept his gaze fixed on the way ahead.

'How far to the house?' shouted William, and Idris glanced back at him.

'Still a way to go,' he said, and William realised it was pointless pressing him to give some idea of time. It was a concept that Idris simply didn't understand. William imagined Mrs Craddock rising from sleep and going to knock on the door of the attic bedroom, only to find William gone. How would he ever explain his absence to her?

There was a last swirl of grey and the fog was gone, as though banished by the gathering light. Now William could see the clifftop stretching ahead of them, already dusted by a gleaming mantle of snow and, off in the near distance, the bleak shape of the house, silhouetted against the rising sun, which was just beginning to appear on the eastern horizon.

'Can't we go any faster?' William pleaded, but Idris shook his head.

'Too slippy,' he said. 'Maggie could fall and hurt herself.'

'But we're running out of time!'

'Not far now. Idris will take n'other short cut!'

'You *did* see her, didn't you?' said William. 'The woman in the circle.'

But Idris shook his head. 'Idris saw nothing,' he insisted, and the tone of his voice suggested that he wasn't going to change his mind about that.

William bit his lip. The snow was gathering force by the second, making it almost impossible to see the way ahead, and it still looked quite a distance to the Rise. What would he say if Mrs Craddock asked him where he'd been? How would he ever explain it? He certainly couldn't tell her the truth.

Now they were hurtling downhill, and in a matter of moments they were on the beach, racing along the flat shoreline, Maggie's hoofbeats muffled by the damp sand. As they moved past a stretch of black rocks, a flight of dark shapes flapped suddenly into the air, crows, startled by the approaching horse. This struck a chord with William. He had seen those birds somewhere before. And the rocks themselves were also strangely familiar, that long run of black stone and then three individual boulders, laid out on the sand, one after the other, two large and one small. But how *could* he know them? He had never been to this beach before. Unless...

And then it came to him. The dream. The recurring dream where he was digging in the sand beside those self-same rocks. If there had been more time, he would have asked Idris to stop so he could have a better look. But they could not afford to waste another moment...

It seemed to take an eternity to cross the remaining space, by which time William had imagined all kinds of disasters: Maggie could slip and break a leg, leaving them stranded; the snow might get so thick that they'd have to stop and wait for assistance; they might meet Seth on horseback, heading out for one of his early morning rides; but finally, finally, they were galloping up the steep and precarious slope that led directly from the beach up to the clifftop, Maggie grunting with the extra effort. They crested the slope and within moments came to the entrance gates and galloped down the path beyond. Before they even reached the front door, Idris pulled Maggie to a halt, grabbed William around the waist and almost threw him to the ground; then he spurred the horse away in the direction of the stables, clearly as reluctant as William to have to answer questions about their outing. William didn't waste any time. He ran around to the back door of the house and let himself in, cringing when he heard a sharp bark from the dining room. He stood for a moment in the scullery, shaking the telltale snow off his jacket and wiping the white flecks from his hair with a piece of old sacking. Once he was sure he'd done enough, he made his way through the kitchen and out to the hallway, meaning to head straight up the stairs to his room, but he froze when he heard a heavy tread on the stairs a couple of flights above, as somebody made their way down.

Mrs Craddock was already up! She must have called at his room and found it empty. He stifled a curse and turned on his heel, heading straight back into the scullery. He stood there for a moment on the verge of panic, unsure of what to do, but then inspiration hit him. He went down on his knees in front of the boiler and started scraping the used coals out from under it into the tin bucket he always used for the task.

A moment later, the door opened and Mrs Craddock came in. She stood there, looking suspiciously down at him.

'What are you doing down yure?' she asked him.

'I . . . couldn't sleep,' he told her, without looking up. 'So I thought I'd make a start on things.'

She sniffed, took a step closer. 'That's not like you,' she observed. 'I usually have to turf you out of that bed.' She studied him for a moment. 'Why this sudden desire to work?'

He shrugged. 'I just . . . thought I would.'

'Your jacket's wet.'

'Er...yes, I...I went to fetch water from the well.'

'Did you now?' She prodded one of the wooden buckets with the toe of her boot. 'So you've already filled the boiler, have you?'

'Er...no.' He paused in what he was doing and turned to look at her. 'It...was snowing too hard,' he said. 'So I thought I'd...just get the fire going first and see if the snow eases off a bit.'

This seemed to amuse her. 'You'd light a fire under an empty boiler?' she sneered. 'That's not a very good idea.'

'Oh, well, there's still a bit of water left in it from yesterday,' he told her. He had no idea if this was true, but luckily she didn't bother to check.

'A bit of snow isn't going to kill you,' she said. 'No sign of Rhiannon yet?'

William shook his head. 'I expect she'll be late this morning,' he said. 'That snow's coming down heavy.'

Mrs Craddock walked to the window and peered out into the back garden.

'This is nothing,' she assured him. 'You wait till proper winter gets yure. The snow lies six foot deep sometimes. You have to dig a path out of the place. This is just a sprinkling.' She considered for a moment. 'Well, finish making up the fire,' she said. 'But don't light it until you've filled that tank properly.'

'Yes, Mrs Craddock.'

'And don't be all day about it.'

She turned and went towards the door and William paused long enough to allow himself a soft sigh of relief. He told himself he'd got away with it. But she paused in the doorway and turned back to look at him. 'You're up to something,' she said. 'Don't think you can hide anything from me, boy. I can read you like a book.'

He gave her what he hoped was an innocent look. 'I'm not sure what you mean, Mrs Craddock. I just . . . wanted to make a start.'

'And I'm Joan of Arc,' she said. She gave him a long, shrewd look. 'I didn't come down with the last shower of rain, you know. You'll need to get up very early in the morning to get one over on me.'

And with that, she turned and walked out of the room, leaving him to wonder exactly how much she knew.

CHAPTER FIFTEEN
A Visitor

Mrs Craddock had been right about the weather. As November tottered to a conclusion, the skies darkened and the snow came down heavier and heavier, until one morning William opened the back door to find a crisp white wall filling the doorway. His first job that day was to bring bucket after bucket of snow into the scullery to throw into the boiler to melt. Then he was issued with a shovel and sent outside to clear a path all the way up to the well. Once that was accomplished, Mrs Craddock instructed him to do the same thing to the long drive that led from the front door to the entrance gates. It was a mammoth task, work that made him sweat despite the bitter cold.

Rhiannon didn't arrive until after midday, and when she got there, she looked half dead with the cold. She had been wading through drifts that came higher than her knees, one hand clutching her rabbit's-foot charm to keep her safe.

William made her sit beside a roaring fire to thaw out, despite the disapproving looks from Mrs Craddock, who seemed to think that the best way for the girl to warm up was to start work. Rhiannon, once she had stopped shivering, told them that her father had announced before she set off that over the past few days production at the quarry had dropped away to almost nothing, and he expected this latest fall to shut things down entirely. Nobody wanted to be the one to inform Seth about that. He was not a man to take such news calmly.

William had told nobody about his discovery in the old chapel. He had nearly confessed it to Rhiannon at one point, but at the last moment, had decided against it. What could a young girl like her be expected to do with such information? And superstitious as she was, she would almost certainly interpret it as the work of demons. Idris had made it clear that he didn't want to know about it, and any time William tried to bring the subject up, Idris steadfastly talked about something else. He seemed to think that even a hint of the truth would be enough to land him in some kind of trouble.

Mrs Craddock would have taken a very dim view of William sharing such 'tittle-tattle' with her, even though she was the biggest gossip around when given the opportunity. Which only left Toby, and William really didn't think he should go making suggestions about what the boy's stepfather might have got up to in secret. But who else was there for him to confide in? Audrina, whom he still glimpsed from time to time? Would it make sense to try to strike up a conversation with a ghost?

On one occasion he'd seen her drifting past the entrance gate. It was broad daylight, just after a heavy fall of snow. She paused for a moment and pointed across the clifftop, as though trying to draw his attention to something, before going silently on her way. When William had trudged over to examine the place where she'd been, he somehow wasn't surprised to discover that she had managed to trespass there without leaving a single footprint in the snow.

Another time, he'd been walking past the large mirror in the hallway, carrying a platter of potatoes to the dining room, and just for an instant he'd seen her hooded face staring at him from the mirror, those unseen eyes burning into him. It had made him jump so violently that he'd dropped the platter, scattering the food all over the floor, and by the time he'd gathered it back up and thought to check the mirror again, only his own harassed features stared back at him. Once again he was struck by the impression that there was something that Audrina wanted him to do. 'Bring him to me,' she'd told him in the chapel. But bring who? Seth? Toby? And bring them where? William never knew where Audrina might turn up next.

The *Gwrach* he didn't see at all, and he was profoundly grateful for that. He would be happy to never see her again as long as he lived.

Soon it was December. If he had thought that the house might be decorated to greet the festive season, he was wrong. Uncle Seth, it seemed, did not approve of such frivolity. He would greet Christmas with the same sullen demeanour with which he marked the rest of the year. There would be no holly boughs, no decorations, no presents, no gatherings of friends or family.

William gave up hope of anything ever changing for the better. It seemed to him that he was doomed to live in this cold, unfriendly house for the rest of his days, without ever fully unravelling its secrets.

But one December afternoon something unexpected happened. It began with the shrill sound of the front doorbell clanging, an event so unusual here that William nearly jumped out of his skin. Mrs Craddock was busy dressing a side of beef for dinner. 'Now who can that be?' she asked William, who was sweeping the kitchen floor. Rhiannon had gone to the back garden to fetch water, so Mrs Craddock threw a look in William's direction and said, 'Get that, will you?'

William set down his broom and went out to the hallway to unlatch the door. Standing on the step was a stout little man wearing a heavy overcoat, a muffler tied tight around his neck and a grey top hat pulled down low over his eyes. In one gloved hand he carried a leather briefcase. On the snow-covered drive behind him stood a coach and horses, a driver sitting at the reins, shivering under a heavy blanket. The visitor had a round, ruddy face and long brown side whiskers. His blue eyes studied William with evident interest.

'Is this the house of Mr Seth Jessop?' he asked quietly.

'It is, sir,' said William. 'May I tell him who's calling?'

'My name is Cadwallader,' said the man, in a rich Welsh accent, 'and you may inform him of that in a moment. But first, would you be so good as to tell me, if there is a young boy staying here, a boy who answers to the name of Master William Jessop?'

William was taken aback. He stared at the man in surprise. It was so long since anyone had used his surname he'd almost forgotten he was actually a member of the Jessop family.

'Er...yes, sir,' he said.

'Splendid,' said the man, smiling. 'And where would I find him?'

'Find him, sir?'

The man looked slightly irritated. 'Yes, *find* him! I have some information that concerns him.'

'Er...but...that's *me*, sir. *I* am William Jessop.'

'You?' Mr Cadwallader stared at him, open-mouthed.

'Yes, sir.'

Now the man looked really confused. He studied William for a moment, appearing to pay particular attention to the uniform he was wearing. 'But...forgive me, aren't you a...a servant?'

'I am, sir. But I am still William Jessop. And I'm the only one by that name you'll find here.'

The man seemed to consider this information for a moment before he spoke again. 'Well, William, if I may call you that, I must tell you that I have been on a merry dance looking for you. Believe it or not, I've been trying to find you for quite some time.'

PART THREE
DECEMBER 1853

CHAPTER SIXTEEN
THE WILL

After that, there was some confusion. William went to find Seth, only to discover that he was in his study at the back of the house, a place where William was never allowed to enter, so he had to tap gently on the oak door and call through, telling his uncle that there was a visitor, a man who called himself Mr Cadwallader, which elicited a muffled curse from within. A moment later, the study door opened an inch or so and Seth peered out, his face a picture of annoyance.

'What the devil does he want?' snarled Seth.

'I do not know, uncle,' said William. 'He is asking to see you. He says he has come all the way from Harlech.'

'Who travels such distances in this weather?' wondered Seth, and when William was unable to give an answer, he added, 'Well, you'd better tell him to come in, I suppose. I'll meet him in the dining room.'

'Yes, uncle,' said William, and he headed straight back to the hallway, where he'd left the stranger. When he got there, the man had removed his hat and scarf and was giving them to Rhiannon, who had returned from the well. 'I wonder if my coachman might be admitted to the kitchen to warm himself up a bit?' asked Mr Cadwallader. 'He's all but frozen solid in his seat, the poor devil.'

'I'll go and ask Mrs Craddock,' said Rhiannon. 'I'm sure it will be all right.'

'Thank you, my dear.'

'Uncle Seth will speak to you in the dining room,' announced William. 'If you'd like to follow me?'

Mr Cadwallader nodded and walked with William along the hallway, studying him with apparent interest. 'How long have you lived here?' he asked quietly.

'Er...three months, sir,' said William.

'I see. And your uncle has you working for him?'

'Yes, sir.'

'What an unusual arrangement.'

As they approached the dining room, the door opened and Toby came out, a book in his hand. He threw a disapproving look at Mr Cadwallader as he went by. 'Banished to my room,' he muttered sourly. 'I'll probably freeze to death up there.' He strode on past, and Mr Cadwallader gave William a puzzled look.

'That's Toby,' said William. 'My cousin.'

He led Mr Cadwallader into the dining room, where they found Uncle Seth standing in front of the fireplace, warming himself. He appraised the visitor as he approached, his expression suggesting that he didn't much like what he saw. Beside him, one of the wolfhounds gave a low, rumbling growl, his hackles rising, but Seth silenced him with a quick tap of his boot. Mr Cadwallader gave a formal bow and then stepped forward, his hand extended to shake, but Seth ignored the gesture.

'Who are you?' he asked bluntly. 'And what's your business here?'

Mr Cadwallader stepped back and smiled politely. 'Did William not give you my name?' he asked.

'He did, and it meant nothing to me.'

Mr Cadwallader reached into his waistcoat pocket and pulled out a small white card, which he handed to Seth. Seth studied it contemptuously.

'Mr Edwyn Cadwallader,' muttered Seth. 'Of Thomas, Jenkins and Hughes, Solicitors.' He handed the card back. 'My father's law firm, if I remember correctly.' He glanced sharply at William. 'And why are you still here?' he snapped. 'Go back to the kitchen and get on with some work.'

William started to leave, but Mr Cadwallader put a hand on his arm to restrain him. 'If it's all the same to you, Mr Jessop, I would really rather William stayed,' he said. 'My business today concerns him.'

Seth looked outraged. 'I fail to see why any business of mine should concern *him*,' he said. 'He's just—'

'Your nephew, is he not?' interrupted Mr Cadwallader, effectively silencing Seth. 'For all that he wears the uniform of a servant.' Then he looked around the room and gestured to the dining table. 'Could we perhaps sit down together, the three of us? It's been quite an arduous journey up here.'

'I'm surprised you made it,' observed Seth. 'Those roads are damned dangerous in this weather. It's a wonder you didn't come to grief.' There was a wistful tone in his voice as though that was exactly what he wished had happened. But he led the way across to the table and he and Mr Cadwallader sat down. William hesitated, but the lawyer indicated the seat beside him and William obediently perched on it, aware of Seth's gaze burning resentfully into him as he did so. 'So what's all this about?' asked Seth.

'As you already know, Mr Jessop, I represent the firm who looked after your late father's estate,' said Mr Cadwallader. 'I'm sure you will recall that, after he passed away, you came to our head office in Harlech to sign some papers.'

'I remember the offices. I don't seem to recall you.'

'I'm fairly new there,' said Mr Cadwallader. 'A junior partner – I took over from old Mr Lawrence when he retired. You will surely remember him? He dealt with all matters relating to your father's estate. The two of them were close friends, I believe.'

'Really?' Seth shrugged, as though it was of no interest to him.

'Well, to the matter in hand...' Mr Cadwallader leaned down to the briefcase, which he had set on the floor beside him. He unclasped it and withdrew a large brown folder. 'I must say, I hadn't expected it to be quite such a trial contacting you,' he said. He straightened up and placed the folder on the table. 'I sent you several letters, none of which was answered.'

'If you sent me letters, then I didn't receive them,' said Seth. 'The post is notoriously bad in these parts. Papers often go astray.'

'Is that right? How very strange. Particularly as the third and final letter was sent by a special courier, who assures me that he personally placed my package into your hands.'

Seth continued to stare straight at the lawyer. 'If the man says that, then he is a damned liar,' he snapped.

'Well, whatever the explanation...when Mr Lawrence retired, he left a list of matters that he wished me to deal with on his behalf – what he described as "unfinished business". I must confess that in all the chaos of my start at the firm, I neglected the list for quite some time. But, when I finally had the opportunity to read through it, I noted that Mr Lawrence had mentioned the demise of your brother, Mr Matthew Jessop. He had made a particular note pertaining to his son, William. So I set about trying to trace the boy. My enquiries eventually led me to a workhouse in Northwich, where I spoke to a lady by the name of Mrs Selby.' He glanced at William. 'I'm sure you're familiar with her,' he commented.

William nodded, but didn't have anything good to say about her, so he held his tongue.

'I must confess that I found the woman rather evasive,' continued Mr Cadwallader, 'particularly when it came to the subject of any provision that Mr Jessop might have left for his son. And then, imagine my surprise, when after some pressing on my part she finally explained that young William had come here to live with you. That was the main point of the three letters I sent to you over the next couple of months, requesting a meeting. What a pity that you didn't receive them! I had hoped to speak to you many weeks ago.' He opened the folder and took out a thick sheath of papers. 'In the end I decided that I had no alternative but to call here in person. My partners at the firm warned me that I should wait until the spring, but I decided that this needed to be dealt with as a matter of some urgency, no matter how inclement the weather. I had, after all, given Mr Lawrence my undertaking that I would settle the matter for him at my earliest convenience. So here I am.' He beamed warmly at Seth, and William decided that he rather liked this man's cheery disposition. It was like a ray of sunshine breaking through the shadows of the old house. But he couldn't help wondering why the lawyer had wanted him to stay in the room for the meeting.

Now Mr Cadwallader slid some of the papers across the table to Seth. 'I'm sure you recognise this,' he said.

Seth barely glanced at it. 'My father's will,' he said. 'What of it?'

Mr Cadwallader took a second bundle from the file and set them in front of himself. 'I have an exact copy here,' he said. 'I should like to draw your attention, if I may, to page fifteen – the place where it deals with your father's bequests.' He glanced at William again. 'Are you familiar with that word, William?' he asked. 'Bequest?'

'No, sir.'

'It means . . . when you bequeath something. When you make provision for somebody. When you leave them something in a will.'

'I see,' murmured William, still mystified.

'Yes, I think we have the general idea,' said Seth, turning the pages. He sounded irritated. 'I really don't see the point in going over all this again. It's a matter of record that my father left me his entire estate.'

'Not quite his *entire* estate,' Mr Cadwallader corrected him. 'I would draw your attention to clause seven, where your father made a bequest to his other son, Matthew: William's father. Shall I read it to you?'

'I imagine you'll do as you see fit,' muttered Seth ungraciously.

Mr Cadwallader smiled politely and then began to read. 'To my son Matthew, I bequeath in perpetuity ten per cent of the sum worth of my estate, this to be claimed and used as he so desires.'

Seth snorted dismissively. 'Well, that was a waste of ink,' he said. 'Matthew had no interest in the quarry. Or in the profits it made. He was, of course, informed about our father's death, but he made no attempt to claim any money. He was too proud to do such a thing. He would never have touched a penny of the old man's estate. Besides –' Seth waved a hand – 'he's dead now, isn't he? Dead and buried. So it's surely irrelevant.'

Mr Cadwallader shook his head. 'May I now, sir, direct your attention to sub-clause Seven A?' he asked. 'You see the little asterisk beside the name "Matthew Jessop"?' Seth nodded. 'And if you would be kind enough to look down to the bottom of the page, you will see there's an addendum, added by William's grandfather and signed by him and Mr Lawrence, as witness to it: "Or his heirs", it says. Do you see that, sir?'

Something happened to Seth's face then. His expression registered neither shock nor surprise, but a look of intense annoyance. It occurred to William then that his uncle had already known about the addendum and had chosen to keep quiet about it.

'But that's...that's ridiculous,' said Seth. 'You cannot seriously be suggesting that this young boy...'

'Matthew Jessop's son and heir,' Mr Cadwallader reminded him, still smiling. 'The law is the law, sir, and your father inserted this addendum only a few weeks before he died. It is of course rather ironic. At the time the will was written, a tenth of your father's estate would not have amounted to so very much, but...given the recent increases in the prices of slate, well...' Again he turned to look at William. 'Ten per cent of a large fortune is still a small fortune...and one well worth having, I would say. And no doubt it's a fortune that will only accumulate as the slate industry continues to prosper. I imagine that you will want to make a claim on the estate, won't you, William?'

William stared at the lawyer in astonishment. He thought he was finally beginning to understand what the man was saying. If William had it right in his own head, it meant that there was money for him in those papers, money that might change his life.

'Sir,' he whispered, 'are you...are you saying that I'm going to be...?'

'Rich, William.' Mr Cadwallader smiled that beaming smile. 'Yes, that's exactly what I'm saying. Oh, you will not have the kind of wealth that your uncle here has at his command, but nevertheless, you will be, by any stretch of the imagination, a prosperous young gentleman ... when you come of age.'

'Age, sir?'

'When you are twenty-one. That is the age when you will inherit your share of the estate.' Now he turned to look back at Seth. 'May I enquire, sir, if you have officially adopted William?' he asked.

'Nothing of the sort,' said Seth. 'Out of the goodness of my heart, I simply agreed to give him a roof over his head ...'

'And employment, it would seem.'

Seth waved a hand as if to dismiss the matter. 'The boy's a valet for my stepson, Toby. Well, he needed something to occupy his time.'

'I see. But you have signed no papers affording you any rights as his legal guardian?'

'No. It was simply a kindly gesture. It seemed the decent thing to do.'

'A most generous offer, I'm sure. Though I would suggest that the arrangement be solemnised in a legal document at the earliest opportunity. Just so William knows where he stands. And ...'

'Yes?' Seth leaned forward in his seat.

'I would question your decision to have your nephew working as a member of staff here. He is, after all, destined to be one of your beneficiaries in the fullness of time. Would it not be more suitable for him to go to school, get himself a decent education? He might prove to be an asset. One day he could even assist you . . .'

Seth's expression hardened. 'I would advise you, sir, to mind your own damned business,' he said. 'What happens in Jessop Rise is my concern and I would thank you to keep your nose out of it.'

Mr Cadwallader's smile never faded. He bowed his head. 'Of course, sir. Forgive me, it was merely a suggestion.' He gathered up his papers and returned them to the folder. 'Well, Mr Jessop, I have imparted the information I came here to deliver. I will leave that copy of the will with you and I shall head back to Harlech. On my return to the office, I shall, however, draw up the paperwork you'll need to make a legal adoption of William and will ensure that it is despatched to you with all speed. I would ask that you sign and return it at your earliest convenience.' He smiled, and put the folder back into the briefcase. 'Now, sir,' he said, 'I wonder if I might be allowed to have a few words with William in private?'

'What would that be in aid of?' growled Seth.

'I just wish to offer him an opportunity to ask any questions he might have about his inheritance,' said Mr Cadwallader. 'Without any pressure.'

Seth got to his feet. 'You may do as you damned well please,' he said. 'I have more important things to think about. I've got an entire quarry standing idle thanks to this hellish weather.' Seth got to his feet and strode across to the door. He opened it, threw a last glare in William's direction and then went out, slamming the door behind him.

Mr Cadwallader waited a few moments and then smiled at William. 'It would seem that this has come as a bit of a shock to you,' he said. 'Did you really have no idea that your grandfather had made such provision for you?'

William shook his head. He felt a sense of unreality surrounding him. He was still trying to come to turns with his unexpected good fortune. He would be rich in a few years' time. And if he had money at his command, who knew what might lie ahead for him? But then he told himself that he would not inherit his fortune for another seven years, far too late to think about putting himself through school. He tried to imagine himself living here under his uncle's cruel command, with all the strange mysteries of the house going on around him, and he told himself that he would most likely go insane long before he was old enough to escape – assuming he survived that long.

He realised that he needed to talk to somebody about his situation, and that he would never have a better opportunity than this.

'Sir, may I speak to you about a private matter?' he murmured.

Mr Cadwallader looked at him in surprise. 'Of course,' he said. 'Something to do with the will?'

William shook his head. 'No, sir. Something else. I...I need to talk to you about my uncle. But you must promise not to say anything to him about what I'm about to tell you.'

Mr Cadwallader looked intrigued. He nodded. 'You have my word on it,' he said. 'What's on your mind?'

William took a deep breath. 'Sir,' he began, 'do you believe in ghosts?'

CHAPTER SEVENTEEN
A CONVERSATION

For a moment Mr Cadwallader looked as though he might be about to laugh, but the earnestness of William's expression must have stopped him.

'No,' he said, calmly. 'I do not believe in ghosts. Do you?'

'I didn't until I came to this house. If you had told me stories of such things back in Northwich, I would have laughed at them! But since I have been here, sir, I have changed my mind.'

Mr Cadwallader frowned. He leaned back in his chair and gazed around the room. 'It's a remote spot,' he reasoned. 'Dark. Shadowy. And after everything you went through with the death of your father, it is little wonder if your imagination is running away with you... It was a factory accident, was it not?'

'Yes, sir, but that has nothing to do with what I have seen here. It is not my father who haunts me. If only that were so.' William paused for a moment, trying to think of the best way to explain what was on his mind. 'Since I have been here, sir, I have seen the ghost of a woman.'

'Have you indeed?'

William nodded. 'I have seen her several times, a cloaked, hooded figure. I cannot be sure, but I have come to believe that it must be the ghost of Audrina, my uncle's wife.'

'Ah.' Mr Cadwallader looked interested. 'Well, of course I am familiar with the story. Around a year ago, wasn't it? Her disappearance was big news in the area at the time, and was widely reported in the local newspapers. No trace of her was ever found; is that not so?'

'That's what I have been told, sir.' William looked intently at Mr Cadwallader. 'May I ask you, do you…do you trust my uncle?'

Mr Cadwallader stared at William for a moment and then blew out a breath of air from between pursed lips. 'That is really not for me to say,' he replied. 'I scarcely know him. Certainly he was very remiss in answering my letters, but in that respect he is sadly not unique. There are, I'm afraid, many people who do not answer their correspondence promptly. That is an annoyance, not a crime.'

'What about his making me work here? You said yourself I should be allowed to go back to school.'

'Er... well, that was only my personal opinion, William. As your guardian, I dare say your uncle must do as he sees fit. May I enquire, though, are you paid for your work here?'

'No, sir, not a penny. Though I *was* given a gold sovereign when I saved my cousin's life, down at the quarry.'

Mr Cadwallader raised his eyebrows at that, but made no comment.

'And I have my suspicions that the boulder that fell that day, sir... it... it might not have fallen by accident. I think perhaps it was meant to kill me. Possibly me and my cousin both.'

Mr Cadwallader looked shocked. 'That's quite an accusation, William!'

'I know,' continued William, 'but I believe it to be the truth. And, you see, sir, I think Audrina... if that is who it really is... I think she's trying to tell me something. I think she wants me to help her.'

'Help her with what?'

'I don't know. I think it might have to do with...' William hesitated, not sure he dared to say more, '...something I... saw...'

'Go on,' Mr Cadwallader prompted him.

'Sir, if I speak of this thing . . . you must promise me that you will not tell my uncle that I have informed you of it. *Please.*'

Mr Cadwallader nodded. 'William, you are my client today, and every lawyer takes an oath of confidentiality. So rest assured, your secret will be safe with me.'

William nodded. He felt reassured. 'Sir, there is an old ruined chapel up on the clifftops. I don't know if it even has a name. A friend told me about something that was hidden there, and I . . . well, I decided to go out early one morning, before the sun came up, to have a look for myself.'

'Did you now?'

'Yes, sir. Well, I found what I was looking for. It was under the floorboards, behind the altar, locked in a wooden casket.'

'William, what on earth are you talking about?'

'Audrina was there too, sir, sitting in one of the pews, watching me . . .'

Now Mr Cadwallader did laugh. 'I'm sorry, but do you have any idea how this sounds?' he snorted.

William nodded. 'Yes, sir, I know it must seem as though I have lost my mind. And for a while, I thought that might be what was happening to me. But I swear to you, the casket *is* there. You only have to look at what's hidden inside it and you will see that I'm telling the truth.'

Mr Cadwallader looked very interested now. 'And what is that?' he asked.

'A body, sir.'

'It must be a very big casket, William!'

'No, sir, not the body of a man. It is that of a . . . a baby.'

There was a long silence, before Mr Cadwallader spoke again. 'William, if you are spinning me some kind of yarn, I must tell you that I am not finding this very funny.'

'It's true, I swear! And I know that my uncle has visited the chapel on at least one occasion to look at what is hidden in that casket. He cried when he looked upon it.'

Mr Cadwallader got up from the table and walked across to the fireplace. He stared into the flames as though deep in thought. 'What you have told me is troubling,' he confessed, 'and I must admit that I have heard rumours about Mr Jessop before today.'

'What rumours, sir?'

'Oh, just . . . tavern gossip. No reason to believe that there's any truth in it. And it would be very unprofessional of me to—'

'Please, sir, I need to know.'

Mr Cadwallader turned back from the fire. He looked uneasy, but he must have seen the desperate expression on William's face and after a few moments' hesitation, he relented. 'I must first insist, William, that this goes no further. Do you understand me? If it were to get out that I had expressed opinions about the son of one of our most valued clients, it would not be treated lightly by my employers. I would almost certainly lose my job.'

William nodded. 'I promise, sir, I will speak of it to nobody. You have my word on that.'

Mr Cadwallader sighed. 'Very well.' He glanced towards the door as though nervous of being overheard, and when he spoke again his voice was little more than a whisper. 'There are certain people who claim that your uncle had a secret mistress, some years after he was married.'

'A mistress, sir?'

'Yes. She was an entertainer of some kind, a dancer at a carnival show, or so I was told.'

At this, a memory flashed into William's mind. The playbill that he'd found in Audrina's room that time, the one that had been hidden behind the dressing table. One of the acts listed there had been some kind of dancer...

no wonder Seth had looked so furious when he saw that playbill!

'It is said that he kept the affair secret from his wife,' continued Mr Cadwallader. 'How these gossips came by their information is only to be guessed at, but...also...'

'Yes, sir?'

'There was one man I spoke to, a colleague, who told me...he told me that Seth Jessop is a man of incredible power in this area. This was when I was despairing of ever getting a reply to my letters. My colleague told me that Mr Jessop is a close friend of the chief law officer of the county, and that one reason Audrina's disappearance was never solved could be that certain people were...paid off.'

'You're saying that—'

'I'm saying nothing! I'm telling you what a colleague who'd had a flagon of ale too many confided in me. That doesn't make it true. But my friend did point out that the law officer in question lives in a fine house, one that would seem beyond the reach of most men of his occupation.'

'My uncle *is* the richest man in the county; he's always boasting of it.'

Mr Cadwallader frowned. 'Even so, we must hold back from speculation, until we have some facts.' He lifted a hand to stroke his chin. 'You swear to me this business with the casket is true?'

'On my word of honour.'

'Well, then it must be investigated. I shall report the matter to the constabulary when I get back to Harlech. I am sure that they will make it a priority.'

'But couldn't you go to the police in Porthmadog?'

Mr Cadwallader shook his head. 'I don't want to risk reporting it here, where it might be brushed under the carpet by your uncle's friends. I'd rather wait until I can speak to men I know to be trustworthy. Say nothing to anyone of our conversation, until we know more. Is that clear?'

'Yes, sir.'

Mr Cadwallader came back to the table and sat down. 'As to the ghostly aspects of your tale, William, I have to confess I do not believe in such phantoms, though I can see that you really are convinced that you have seen things beyond your understanding. But we must stick to what we can prove. For the time being, I can only advise you to keep your head down and try to stay out of trouble.'

William didn't like the sound of that. 'Why do you say this, sir?'

'It's only that I had a feeling, when I was speaking with your uncle, that he was being insincere when he expressed surprise at hearing of his father's bequest to you. Does he strike you as the sort of man who would miss a detail like that?'

William shook his head. 'I'd say he's the sort of man who wouldn't miss a trick. I think he knew about it.'

'I have to admit that is my feeling too,' admitted Mr Cadwallader. 'Though of course I could not challenge him on it.' He thought for a moment. 'When I spoke to Mrs Selby at the workhouse, she told me that she had written to your uncle to inform him of your situation...'

'But that's not true! She told me that *he* wrote to *her*. She showed me the letter, sir. It was a complete surprise to her.'

Mr Cadwallader nodded. 'Interesting. So he sought you out and asked you to come to this house?'

'Yes, sir.'

'There's an old expression, William: "Keep your friends close and your enemies closer." It could just be that Mr Jessop is following that advice.'

'But...I don't understand. I'm not his enemy; I'm his nephew.'

Mr Cadwallader shrugged. 'I take your point,' he said. 'But to some men, anyone who threatens to take away what they have…even if it be only ten per cent of their worth…may, through no fault of their own, be perceived as an enemy. There are men in this world who put profit above any other consideration. I looked into Mr Jessop's eyes back then and I saw a ruthless fellow who would let nothing stand in his way.'

'Are you saying that I'm in danger?'

Mr Cadwallader lifted a hand as if to slow things down. 'Let's not get ahead of ourselves,' he suggested. 'Look, the sooner I am on my way, the sooner I shall be back in my own neck of the woods, where I can report what you have told me. If there *are* human remains hidden in that church – and God help you, William, if you have told me a lie – then Mr Jessop will have to explain how they came to be there and why he has not reported them to the proper authorities. If there is any suggestion that he may intend you harm, William, then I shall see to it that you are removed from here and taken to a safe place, as soon as possible.'

'Oh, sir, that would be—'

'But you must appreciate I cannot do anything about it at this moment,' Mr Cadwallader interrupted. 'I wish I could, but I have to be sure that you have told me the truth on this matter. And that will only be established once somebody has visited the old chapel of which you spoke.' He put a hand on William's shoulder. 'Trust me, I shall do everything I can to resolve matters to your advantage as quickly as possible.' He picked up and secured his briefcase. 'Now I suggest that I get on my way, before we arouse suspicion. Walk with me.'

They got up from their seats, went to the door and stepped out into the hallway, then walked to the front entrance in silence, where they found the coachman waiting for them, looking a little warmer than when he'd arrived. Rhiannon appeared carrying Mr Cadwallader's hat, muffler and overcoat. He set down his briefcase and put them on, fastening the muffler tightly around his neck.

The front door opened and Uncle Seth came in. He was dressed in a thick overcoat, and William saw that he was wearing his leather riding boots. 'Ah, there you are, Cadwallader,' he said. 'I was beginning to think that you had decided to spend the evening here.'

'Oh no, I . . . merely took the opportunity to, er . . . fully explain a few legal details to William,' said the lawyer warily. 'I wanted to be sure he'd understood everything perfectly.'

'I'm sure William knows exactly what's involved,' said Seth icily. He forced an insincere smile, then turned back to Mr Cadwallader. 'At any rate, I've decided that I'd be a poor host indeed if I let you set off for Harlech without accompanying you at least part of the way. It's already getting dark out there. I've just had my horse saddled up so I can ride alongside you.'

Mr Cadwallader's smile faded. 'Oh, you . . . really mustn't trouble yourself,' he protested. 'I . . . have every confidence in my coachman.'

'On a day like this?' Seth chuckled. 'That road is like a frozen pond in places. There's many a carriage come to grief going over that top road, in finer conditions than today. And I know the way down better than anyone. I'll feel much happier if you allow me to guide you back, at least until you're over the worst of it.'

'Please, there really is no need—'

'I insist,' said Seth, looking intently into Mr Cadwallader's eyes, and William suddenly had a bad feeling in the pit of his stomach. He wanted to say something, but couldn't seem to find words. Mr Cadwallader had little option but to nod his assent and turn towards the door, accompanied by his coachman. Seth whistled then and a couple of lean grey shapes came padding down the corridor from the direction of the dining room. The wolfhounds. They loped out into the icy twilight, and now William was convinced that something was very wrong indeed.

'Mr Cadwallader!' he exclaimed. The lawyer turned back to look at him.

'Yes, William?" he said quietly.

'Be . . . careful out there.'

The lawyer nodded, and then he and the coachman went through the doorway. Seth stood for a moment, looking at William, a sardonic smile on his lips, and then he turned away and followed the others outside. Rhiannon closed the door after him. She turned to look at William excitedly.

'Well,' she exclaimed, 'what was that all about?'

CHAPTER EIGHTEEN
TRAGEDY

After Mr Cadwallader's coach had left, William explained to Rhiannon and Mrs Craddock what the lawyer had just told him. Their attitudes changed instantly. Suddenly it was as though Mrs Craddock could no longer bring herself to issue him with any orders. He wanted to tell her that he wasn't different, not at all, that he was still prepared to do whatever he was told, but it was as though she had somehow become another person entirely. 'Would you mind awfully fetching me that knife, William?' she asked him at one point. And a little later on, 'I was wondering if you wouldn't mind making up the fires in the bedrooms? If it's not too much trouble.'

Rhiannon didn't seem able to even speak to him or cast so much as a look in his direction. It was most peculiar, as though the mere promise of money had somehow made him a different person entirely – and it was useless to tell her that he wouldn't be getting a penny until he was twenty-one. She seemed to regard him now as somebody who should be giving the orders, not taking them.

Then Toby appeared from his room and demanded to know what the visitor had wanted, and William had to explain everything to him. Toby's expression was one of amazed delight, his eyes getting bigger and bigger as though they might pop out of his skull at any moment.

'You lucky bounder!' he exclaimed at last. 'So it seems you are going to be a proper gentleman, just like me. Well, it would appear that congratulations are in order, cousin!' He slapped William heartily on the back and announced that tonight, William would sit at the dinner table instead of waiting on it. And with that he marched off to sit by the fire with his book. But William told himself that he should wait until his uncle returned before making any assumptions.

Darkness soon fell, and there was no sign of Seth. William paced agitatedly around the house, trying to occupy himself with whatever bits of work he could persuade Mrs Craddock to assign him, but his mind kept going back to what Mr Cadwallader had said to him.

'*There's an old expression, William. "Keep your friends close and your enemies closer."*'

There was no doubt in William's mind that Seth *did* mean him harm. He was convinced now that the incident at the quarry had been no accident. He reminded himself that Mr Cadwallader had promised to tell the police about what William had discovered in the chapel, but it would surely take time to get men out to such a remote spot and it would be tomorrow afternoon at the earliest before anything could be achieved. Who knew what Seth might accomplish by then? He could feel fear stirring in the pit of his stomach, like a fist clenching and unclenching itself.

Dinnertime came and still Uncle Seth had not returned, so it was decided to go ahead without him. William carried a platter of food into the dining room, only to be told by Toby to leave the rest to 'the servants' and to take a seat beside him.

'I . . . I'm really not sure I should do that,' William told him. 'Uncle Seth might not like it.'

'Nonsense, cousin. What are you afraid of? Now that he knows you're to be a partner in the family business, he's sure to want you to be treated with proper respect.'

William declined to tell Toby that he suspected Seth had already known about the bequest and had kept quiet about it. He reluctantly complied with Toby's invitation, and as the food appeared in front of him, he began to eat, cautiously at first. But his hunger soon won out and he had a lot of lost time to make up for. He loaded his plate with food, hoping that Seth wouldn't suddenly appear and order him to stop.

'So what will you do with your money, when you finally get it?' Toby asked him, and William had to admit that one thing was uppermost in his mind.

'I'd really like to go back to school,' he said.

Toby looked horrified. 'Is that the best thing you can think of?' he asked. 'School? Oh dear.'

'I think it's really important,' insisted William. 'And it was my father's dearest wish that I be properly educated. But the problem is, if I have to wait until I'm twenty-one, then I'll be too old.'

'Oh, I expect something can be arranged,' said Toby cheerfully. 'If that's what you really want, I imagine Seth will agree to advance you some of your money until you come of age.' He thought for a moment. 'And if he won't, well then, I will.'

William stared at his cousin. 'But you don't have *your* money yet.'

'Not my inheritance. But I do have some savings, money my mother left me when I was young. Seth invested it for me. I'd just have to ask him for some.'

'You'd...do that for me?' cried William.

'Well, let's be honest, William – if it hadn't been for you, I'd have been flattened by that boulder back at the quarry. You saved my life that day.' William was surprised to hear Toby sounding so different to his usual manner – contrite, almost friendly. Toby looked thoughtful. 'Look, we didn't get off to a good start when you first arrived here,' he admitted, 'but I see now that I was wrong about you. To tell the truth, I feared at first that you might be a rival.'

'What do you mean?'

Toby looked thoughtful. 'When all is said and done, you are a Jessop, with the same blood as Seth. It occurred to me that he might see you as a better heir to his fortune than I. He's never really got along with me. Oh, he was happy to have my mother's money and the respect that would bring him. I was just something that came along with the deal. He has made it clear that he has no fondness for me, and for that matter I have to confess that I have no interest in his infernal quarry. When I come of age, I shall be happy to leave that side of things to him. But I shall have the house, the estate, the Ransome name and all that goes with it.' He smiled at William. 'And I'm glad that you shall have a small share of Seth's fortune. You deserve that much.'

They ate in silence for a while.

'Has it ever occurred to you that something bad is going on here?' asked William cautiously.

Toby looked at him in surprise. 'What do you mean?' he asked.

'It goes back to that first night I was here. The woman I told you about, the one on the clifftop path . . .'

Toby looked wary. 'Not that again,' he murmured. 'Just when we were getting along so well.'

'No, listen to me,' William urged him. 'Whether you like it or not, Toby, I *have* seen a woman, several times. And . . . well, surely you know who it is?'

Toby looked uncomfortable now. 'Yes,' he said. 'It's all anyone talks about here. The *Gwrach*. I know all about the legend. And, I'll admit, there are things I too cannot explain. I was here the night your grandfather died. I must have been around your age, I suppose. The noise of it! A horrible wailing that seemed to come from all directions. Mrs Craddock kept saying it was just the wind playing tricks, but I didn't believe her for one moment. It sounded like something not of this earth.'

'Oh no,' said William. 'No, I don't think—'

'But let's not talk about such things,' said Toby. 'It puts me in a sour mood.' He seemed to make an obvious attempt to change the subject. 'I've decided that when I inherit, I'm going to travel,' he said. 'I've a longing to see the Americas. I've read that there are prairies there so vast it can take weeks to cross them, even on horseback. And there are buffalo...millions of them.' He looked around the dining room. 'It'll make a change from this dull place, that's for sure. I can't wait to get away. I've often suggested to Seth that he might like to visit the Continent and take me with him, but nothing shifts him from here. It's as though he's taken root.'

'I think there's a reason he cannot leave,' said William.

'Oh really? What's that?'

'It is what we were just talking about,' insisted William. 'The woman I've seen...'

Toby frowned. 'William,' he said, 'I thought I told you—'

'You realise it's not the *Gwrach*, don't you?'

'Well, who else could—'

'Toby, I believe it's your mother.'

Toby stared at him in dull surprise. 'No,' he said. 'No, that's ridiculous. My mother is . . . You're saying my mother is some kind of . . . ghost?'

'I know it sounds mad. But you must be able to accept, after all this time, that perhaps she *is* dead. And you told me yourself that people have tried to tell you that they have seen her. I believe her spirit haunts this place. That's who I have seen, not the *Gwrach*. For some reason she has made herself known to me.'

'But why would she? If it really were my mother, why wouldn't she come to me, her own son? Why choose you, a stranger, instead?'

'I'm not sure. Perhaps because I am an outsider here. Because she saw something in me that she recognised. But I really think that she wants—'

He broke off as the door opened and Seth strode into the room with the two wolfhounds trailing after him. He looked dirty and dishevelled, as though he'd been rolling around in the mud. The dogs were equally grimy. They made a beeline for the fireplace and settled themselves down in the warmth, while Seth took off his long coat and flung it over the back of an armchair. Then he sauntered across to the table and stood for a moment, his hands on his hips. 'Well, here's a pleasant scene,' he observed. 'Making yourself comfortable, nephew?'

'I invited him to join me,' explained Toby. 'I thought now that's he's going to be a partner in the family business, it was only right.'

'A partner?' Seth shot William a fierce glare. 'What have you told him? You've been promised a sum of money. That's hardly the same thing.'

William sat there feeling decidedly uncomfortable under his uncle's gaze. 'That is what I was told,' he insisted.

'What utter nonsense!' snapped Seth. 'You are to inherit a thousand pounds on your twenty-first birthday. That doesn't make you a partner!'

Toby looked at William, clearly confused. 'But...I thought you said it was to be a percentage,' he cried. 'Ten per cent of the estate, you said.'

'That's what Mr Cadwallader told me,' William assured him.

But Seth was shaking his head. 'No, nephew. You've clearly misunderstood. I *thought* you looked confused! There's no percentage mentioned anywhere. A lump sum of one thousand pounds is what is actually set out in the will. Which will be yours on your twenty-first birthday, no doubt about it. It's a considerable sum for one so young. Not that you've done anything to earn it, of course. Simply by being the child of my long-lost brother, you are deemed worthy in the eyes of the law, and I must admit that doesn't sit right with me. But a contract is a contract, so it shall be honoured.'

William glared at him. 'Go and fetch your copy of the will,' he insisted. 'We'll soon see what it says.'

'There's no need,' Seth told him, with a wave of his hand. 'I know exactly what the bequest is, even if you don't. In fact I intend to pass it on to my solicitors tomorrow, to make sure that there can be no mistake. Oh, don't worry, nephew, that money will be yours. In the fullness of time...'

'What's that supposed to mean?' asked Toby, puzzled.

Seth looked at William, his expression one of innocence. 'Well, after all, it's seven years before you're of age to inherit. Who knows what might happen in that time?' He turned to look at Toby. 'And you, boy, even *you* still have another three years to wait, so I wouldn't go getting too comfortable if I were you. What's the old saying? There's many a slip, twixt cup and lip!' He stepped up to the table, helped himself to a glass and filled it full of red wine from a stoneware jug. Then he took a generous gulp of the contents.

'William was just saying he'd like to go back to school,' said Toby. 'I was thinking, surely we could help him with that?'

'Oh, you were *thinking*, were you?' said Seth mockingly. 'That must have been a new experience for you, Toby. You know my feelings about school – a waste of time and money.'

'Yes, but William wants to—'

'Enough!' snapped Seth.

'You're in a strange mood tonight,' observed Toby. 'Why are you . . . covered in mud? It looks as if you've been rolling around in the dirt.'

Seth chuckled. 'That's pretty much what I have been doing,' he said. 'Or at least in the snow.' He drained his glass and refilled it to the brim. 'It's coming down pretty heavy out there.'

William swallowed a chunk of meat with difficulty. 'Did . . . did Mr Cadwallader go on his way safely?' he asked.

Seth sat down at the table, directly opposite William. He reached out a dirty hand and took a lamb chop from a platter. 'You seem very concerned about that solicitor,' he said. 'I wonder what the two of you were discussing just before he left? I saw you through the window from the garden. The two of you seemed to be as thick as thieves.

Chattering away, you were.' Seth took a large bite of the rare meat. A rivulet of blood trickled down his chin. 'Well, I'm afraid he won't be doing any more chattering.'

'What do you mean?' asked William, his anxiety mounting. He let a half-eaten sausage drop back onto his plate. 'What are you saying?'

Seth shook his head. 'That coachman of his didn't have a clue. Not a damned clue. I warned him the road was dangerous. You heard me, didn't you, nephew? I told him it was like a frozen pond out there. But did he listen to me? Oh no.'

William stared at Seth. He felt numb.

'I think he must have misinterpreted what I said,' continued Seth, his mouth full of meat. 'You see, I warned him to go to his *right*, but for some unknown reason he did exactly the opposite.' He glanced at Toby. 'You know that place where the road is very steep and it overhangs the deep gully?'

'By the stream?' offered Toby.

'Yes. Except of course that the stream is frozen over now. At any rate, the coachman steered the wrong way, the wheels slipped on the ice and the carriage swung out over the edge. The whole damned thing overturned and tumbled down into

257

the gully – coach, horses, the lot. That's a thirty-foot drop if it's an inch.' Seth shook his head, as though picturing the scene in his head. 'Even then, they might have survived if they hadn't had that damned hurricane lamp hanging off the side. I'd put it there because I thought it would help light the way. It smashed, of course, and the whole thing went up like a torch.'

William opened his mouth to say something, but no words came out.

'It's a shame,' continued Seth, 'because even after the fall they were still alive down there... judging from the screams I heard.' He took a last bite of his chop and flung the bone to the dogs, who fought over it noisily. 'Of course I rode straight on to Porthmadog for help, but... well, by the time I managed to get back with some men to help me, there really wasn't much left to salvage.' He reached out and took a sausage from the platter, then sniffed at it thought-fully. 'What *was* left of them smelled rather like this.' He took a bite of the sausage and chewed hungrily. 'Such a pity.'

'No!' William's eyes filled with tears and he bowed his head over his plate. His whole body was trembling.

'Oh, come along now, nephew,' said Seth. 'It's not as if

you *knew* the man. You only met him for the first time today.'

'I barely even got to see him,' complained Toby. 'That's typical. A stranger calls to the house and I don't even get introduced! And now he's dead. What was he like, William?'

William tried to speak, but his voice came out as a strangled sob.

'What was that?' asked Seth, smiling coldly.

William managed to get a hold of himself. 'He was decent,' he gasped. 'He said...he said he would help me.'

'Help you with what?' asked Toby, mystified. But William was already getting up from the table. He started towards the door.

'It is very unfortunate,' Seth called after him. 'But only a madman would risk coming up here by coach at this time of year. I *did* warn him.'

Something seemed to explode in William's chest, filling it with a surge of anger. He turned abruptly on his heel and came marching back to confront Seth. '*You* did it!' he cried. He pointed to the hearth. 'You used the dogs to drive that coach over the edge. That's why you took them with you.'

Seth looked amused by this. 'What nonsense!' he said. 'It was an accident, William. Why would I do a thing like that?'

'Because you didn't want him to go asking questions!' William knew he was saying too much, but he somehow couldn't stop himself. The words were pouring out of him. 'You ... you have secrets, uncle. I know you have! And you've realised that I am on to you. You were afraid that I might have told Mr Cadwallader too much.'

'What's he talking about?' asked Toby.

'I haven't the faintest idea,' Seth assured him. He took another generous swig from his glass. 'He's rambling.'

'I know *everything*,' yelled William, stabbing a finger into his uncle's chest. 'I know what went on when you were married to Audrina.'

'What does he mean?' pleaded Toby.

'Nothing,' said Seth dismissively, but his expression was venomous. 'He's raving. The shock must have affected his brain.'

'There's nothing wrong with my brain,' William assured him. 'You think you've got away with it, don't you? But I will tell everyone about what you've done. I will tell—'

He broke off with a yelp of pain as Seth sprang suddenly to his feet and swung an open hand against the side of William's head, knocking him to the floor. William lay there, his head spinning. Seth stood over him, his hands bunched into fists.

'You don't know what you're talking about, boy,' he growled. 'And if I hear another word from you, I swear I shall beat you to within an inch of your life.'

William lay there, gasping for breath, his face still stinging from the blow.

Toby was up out of his seat now and hurrying around the table to try to help William. 'Why did you hit him?' he asked Seth. 'Can't you see he's upset about the accident?'

'Step away from him,' said Seth. 'Unless you want a taste of what he's already had.'

'But what was he saying?' insisted Toby. 'About my mother?'

'He was saying nothing of any worth,' said Seth. 'Lies. Gossip he's picked up from the servants, most likely.' He reached down and yanked a still-dazed William back to his feet. 'You're coming with me,' he snarled. 'We'll put you somewhere where you can cool off.'

'Seth, please let me speak to him!' cried Toby, stepping forward, but Seth pushed him roughly aside and frogmarched William to the door.

'Now…' he murmured through gritted teeth as he reached for the handle. 'Now we'll settle this matter once and for all.'

CHAPTER NINETEEN
CONFESSION

They burst into the hallway, nearly colliding with Rhiannon, who was bringing another plate of bread to the table. She stared at the two of them open-mouthed as they went by her. 'What's going on?' she asked in dismay, but Seth ignored her.

'Mrs Craddock!' he roared. She appeared from the direction of the kitchen, looking understandably worried.

'Why, whatever's the matter, sir?' she asked him.

'I need your keys,' said Seth, waving his free hand at her. 'Quickly, woman, I haven't got all night.'

'Sir, I think you're hurting the boy...'

'When I want your opinion, I'll make a point of asking for it. Now give me those damned keys!'

She managed to fumble the large bunch from her belt and handed them to him, whereupon he pushed William towards the staircase and the two of them started up.

'But what on earth has the boy done?' cried Mrs Craddock.

'Mind your own business,' Seth advised her.

'Where are you taking me?' protested William, shaking his head in an attempt to dispel the dizziness.

'You're going to your room, so we can discuss this matter in private,' Seth told him. He pushed William hard in the back, nearly throwing him off his feet. He glanced back to ensure that they were now out of Mrs Craddock's hearing. 'Now, tell me,' he said quietly, 'what were you and Cadwallader talking about? What were you saying to him?'

'Nothing,' protested William. 'He was just telling me—'

'About the will! Yes, yes, you really expect me to believe that?'

'Well, I—'

'You had to go snooping, didn't you? You couldn't just accept what you had here. I gave you a home, a roof over your head, and this is how you repay me.'

'You only brought me here because you knew about that clause in the will,' snapped William. 'You thought if you had me close, you could keep me from finding out the truth.'

'Did Cadwallader tell you that?'

'No. I worked it out for myself.'

'Clever boy, aren't you? Too clever for your own damned good.'

They were moving along the first-floor landing now, William looking desperately around for some way of escape.

'You can't just lock me in my room,' William told him. 'You'll have to let me out some time. And when you do...'

'And when I do, what then?' Seth gripped his shoulder and propelled him towards the next set of stairs.

'I'll tell everyone that you killed Mr Cadwallader.'

Seth laughed at that. 'You think they'll believe *you*? There's no proof at all. The conditions were terrible and the carriage went over the edge. It was an accident, pure and simple.' They reached the top of the stairs and went along the second-floor landing.

'But we know that's not true, don't we? Why would you take the dogs with you, unless—' William broke off with a yelp of pain as Seth slapped him hard across the face.

'You will learn to hold your tongue,' he said quietly, 'or you will endure the consequences.' Again he pushed William roughly onwards. They started up the last flight of stairs.

'You'd like that, wouldn't you?' gasped William. 'You want me to be silent. But what if I refuse to keep my mouth shut? What will you do then?'

They crossed the final landing to William's room. Seth thrust him inside, then followed, closing the door behind him. He searched through the bunch of keys until he found the right one, pushed it into the lock and turned it, leaving the bunch hanging there. He spun around to face William.

'Nephew, I'm warning you,' he said. 'Be careful how you answer my next question. Will you be quiet, or do you intend to go telling others of your suspicions?'

'I will not be silent,' William told him. 'The truth will come out.'

'Then you leave me no option but to silence you.'

'Is that what happened to Audrina?' asked William. 'Did *she* say things you didn't like? Or did she find out about the other woman?'

Seth's eyes bulged and he actually took a step back, as though William had punched him. 'You...how...how do you know about *her*?' he whispered.

'Everyone knows,' William assured him. 'That's what Mr Cadwallader told me. It's the gossip in every alehouse in the county.'

'No.' Seth shook his head. 'No, you're lying.'

William shook his head. 'He said it was common knowledge that you were carrying on with another woman behind your wife's back. The woman I saw on that playbill...a dancer from a cheap carnival.'

Seth stepped closer and grabbed William's lapels in his hands. He pulled him up close, so close that William could smell his meaty breath. 'Be careful what you say about her, boy. Her name was Carys and I loved her.'

'Perhaps you did,' said William, glaring back at him. 'But you had a wife, didn't you? Which must have made things awkward. Is that why Audrina ran away, because she found out about the two of you? Because she—' William broke off. Seth's face had contorted into an expression of misery. He let go of William and stepped back, lifting a hand to his face. And suddenly that recurring image came into William's head. The image from the dream he'd had a few times now, the same stretch of beach he and Idris had passed on their way back from the ruined chapel, a place where carrion crows gathered as though sensing what lay beneath the sand. And suddenly, horribly, he understood exactly what was hidden down there...and he also knew what had happened to Audrina. He knew it with a certainty that shocked him. 'But...she...didn't run away, did she?' he whispered. 'She never left. She's...buried on the beach. You...you *killed* her, didn't you?'

Seth turned away now, covering his face with his hands. His shoulders shook as he strove to control his anguish. 'You wouldn't understand,' he whispered. 'How could you? You're just a boy. You know nothing of the ways of the world.' He turned back again and William was shocked to see that his uncle's eyes were brimming with tears. 'I first saw Carys at a carnival in Porthmadog. She was dancing the tarantella. The way she moved...I...I'd never seen anyone like her before. And then our eyes met for a moment and...and I knew right there and then she was the one, that I would have no rest until she was mine.' He clawed at the collar of his shirt as though it was too tight. 'But...I was already married to Audrina, you see. We'd been married for more than two years.' He shook his head. 'I knew it was wrong, but...I was like a man possessed. I couldn't be without Carys! And at the same time, I wasn't going to give up Audrina's estate and everything that went with that...the respect it has given me, this fine house, the land. Try to understand, William, our family were poor when I was a boy. We came up from nothing! Your grandfather made the quarry profitable, yes, but my marriage to Audrina brought me something no amount of money could ever buy: status. Respectability. I would have been a fool to throw all that aside.'

'So you saw this woman in secret?'

Seth lifted a fist in front of William's face. 'I warned you not to speak of her like that! Carys was . . . the best thing I ever had. The finest thing. You're just a child; you can't know what it means to love somebody as I loved her. So yes, we . . . we saw each other in secret. I led a double life. And then, a year ago . . . she found herself with child . . .'

'The casket in the chapel!' William realised. 'The baby was *hers*.'

Again Seth stared at him in disbelief. 'You . . . you *know* about the casket? How can you know?'

'I have seen it,' said William.

'But how? Tell me how!'

'Idris saw you there one day, looking under the altar. And crying. He told me about it and I decided to go and see for myself. I wanted to see what could make a cruel man like you cry.'

Now Seth looked horrified. 'So you broke the casket open?'

'No. I was given the key . . .'

'What do you mean? Mrs Craddock is the only one with a key. How dare you steal it from her?'

'I was given the key,' William assured him. 'But not by Mrs Craddock.'

'Everything you say condemns you,' said Seth. 'I can't think of a single reason why I shouldn't silence you.'

'You've already tried to do that once, haven't you? That day at the quarry. That was no accident. I wonder how much you paid somebody to bring down that rock, even though you must have known there was every chance it would hit Toby too.'

Seth studied him. 'Clever,' he murmured. 'Clever boy. Oh, you have it all worked out, don't you? And Toby...' Seth sneered. 'Do you think I care what happens to *him*? He's not even my own child. I would put him away without a moment's hesitation. I would put him down like a dog.'

He looked at his hands, as though imagining doing exactly that. 'Yes, I engineered the accident. After you got into Audrina's room, it occurred to me that you might put two and two together. But the attempt failed. And when Cadwallader turned up, I realised that you would tell him of your suspicions. That's your nature, isn't it, boy? You'll keep pushing and pushing until the truth comes out, won't you? And I cannot afford to let that happen. How can I let you live, knowing what you know? You should have kept your nose out, boy. You should have accepted your fate and got on with things.'

William glanced desperately around the room, telling himself he must keep his uncle talking, at least until an opportunity to escape presented itself.

'Did you . . . did you kill the baby?' he whispered.

'No!' whispered Seth, horrified by the suggestion. 'No, I would never have harmed a hair on his head. He would have been my true son and heir. It was an accident. He died in childbirth. Baby and mother both.' More tears trickled down Seth's gaunt cheeks. 'It had to be done in secret, you see. I . . . I couldn't let Carys have the child anywhere near the Rise. Word would have got out. So a midwife called to the house where she was staying, a house I rented for her, far from Porthmadog, away from prying eyes. The woman was recommended to me by a friend, and she certainly charged enough for her services . . . but –' he shook his head – 'the baby was in a difficult position, she said. He was too long without air. And . . . and Carys had lost so much blood. It was everywhere! She just . . . she just slipped away from me.'

Seth shook his head and extended a hand as though he was reliving the moment. 'What could I do?' he groaned. 'What choice did I have? I buried Carys, and I suppose I should have buried the baby's corpse too, but I couldn't bring myself to do that. He was unbaptised, I couldn't let him lie all alone in unconsecrated ground. So I hid him in the chapel where I could visit in secret. And I swore I would start again. I would be the good husband I had always meant to be, before I met Carys, before madness overtook me. I would make everything right between my wife and me. But... then... then Audrina discovered what had happened.'

William was still looking around for inspiration. 'How did she... find out?' he asked.

'The midwife,' explained Seth. 'I had sworn her to secrecy and paid her handsomely to forget what had happened, but... she must have confided in her husband, and he'd seen a way to make even more money out of it. If he'd come to me, I could have paid him off, but instead the fool went to my wife and she gave him money for the information...' He shook his head, wiped his eyes on the back of his sleeve. 'She was furious... and she threatened to tell others. She was going to shame me. I... couldn't let people know what had happened. You must see that. I'd have been ruined...'

'So what really happened to Audrina?' whispered William.

Seth walked to the far side of the room and stared at the bunch of keys hanging from the lock. William took the opportunity to glance quickly around, searching for a possible weapon. The only thing here was the collection of animal skulls that Idris had gifted him over the past months. Even in the heat of the moment, he noted that once again the skulls were not as he'd left them. Somebody had arranged them into a perfect circle on the table. He took a step towards them, but then Seth turned back to face him and William froze in his tracks. But not before he'd noticed one tiny detail. The first skull that Idris had given him – the crow's skull – was not on the table with the rest.

'I sent Audrina a note,' said Seth, 'asking for a chance to explain everything. I suggested that we meet down on the beach, a favourite walk of ours. She agreed. It was a fine summer evening with a beautiful sunset. It was just the two of us, nobody else for miles. She had brought a lantern to light our way. I . . . explained that now Carys was dead, I had come to my senses and so the two of us could start afresh. I begged her to forget what I had done and give me a another chance. I promised her I would be the perfect husband, kind, attentive . . .' He shook his head. 'But Audrina wouldn't listen. She started telling me what was going to happen. How she would make sure that everyone in the county knew what I had done. How I had betrayed her trust. She told me that when she was finished, I'd be shamed in the eyes of all who knew me. Nobody would ever want to do business with me again. I would be exposed for what I was: an adulterer – worse still, a man who had caused the death of his mistress and her... bastard.' He gasped. 'That was the word that made me snap,' he confessed. 'She said it and suddenly my head seemed to fill with a raw red heat. I reacted. I lashed out. In an instant Audrina lay on the sand before me, still holding her lantern. I had snapped her neck like a twig.'

William took another look at the table of skulls, but knew that Seth would intercept him before he was even halfway to it. He told himself not to panic, that he would think of something. He slipped his right hand into the pocket of his coat, intending to search for anything he might use as a weapon, and he felt a shock jolt through him as his fingers touched a hard, smooth shape in there; a familiar shape. The crow's skull. His hand closed instinctively around it. Audrina was still trying to help him. He reminded himself to keep Seth talking.

'So you... you buried her on the beach?' he whispered.

Seth nodded. 'I left her lying where she had fallen and I went to the stables for a shovel. Nobody saw me; I made sure of that. Idris was out riding that damned horse and Toby was confined to his bed with a fever. I went back to the place where she lay and I buried her deep. Nobody will ever find her, for nothing marks the spot where she lies.'

'I have seen it,' said William, and he saw again how Seth's eyes widened in surprise. 'I could take somebody to it now. I could point to the very spot.'

Seth scoffed. 'How could you? It happened long before you ever came here. Nobody knows where she is.'

'I know,' said William. 'I have seen the place. There's a line of black rocks, two large ones and a small one. She lies a few feet in front of that. Audrina showed me where it was.'

Now Seth's face registered a new expression: a mixture of incredulity and fear. 'What are you talking about?' he whispered. 'That's . . . not possible.'

'Oh, but it is, uncle. I have seen your wife many times since I came here. I saw her the very first night I arrived, out on the clifftop path. I didn't know at the time it was her, but now I am sure of it. And you know that her ghost haunts this place, you and Toby both.'

Seth shook his head. 'You're raving,' he snarled.

'I don't think so. I remember that day we were coming back from the quarry in the growler. I saw your face when you thought something was following us in the fog. You were terrified.'

'Oh, but that...that is...the *Gwrach*. And I didn't see anything. But I heard her calling out behind us...the same sound I heard the night my father died. Oh, there are some who would dismiss it as superstitious nonsense, but there are many who have seen her.'

'I am not talking about the *Gwrach*. I am talking about your wife, Audrina. She is still trying to tell people about what happened to her. She was at the old chapel when I found the casket. She's the one who gave me the key to open it – just as she unlocked the door to her room that time you found me in there. She wants me to help her, and I intend to try.'

'Audrina can have nothing to say to you from beyond the grave,' muttered Seth. 'Such things are not possible.'

'But you know they are! You saw the writing on the paper in her room. Who do you think did that?'

'You, of course! You, trying to convince me of something that simply cannot happen. Audrina is dead and buried. I made sure of that.'

'I tell you, uncle, she may be dead, but her shadow still walks the earth.'

Seth shook his head. 'If that is true, then she will have seen what her passing has done to me,' he said. 'Since her death,

I have spent as little of her money as possible. I have dismissed staff from the estate and cut everything back to the bone. I have spent hours locked in my study, trying to find ways to spend less and less of her inheritance.'

'Guilt,' sneered William. 'You are a murderer, uncle. Don't expect me to feel sorry for you. You killed your wife.'

'And in a moment, boy, you shall surely join her,' snarled Seth. He started forward with deadly intent and William steeled himself, tightening his grip on the skull in his pocket.

'Please, uncle,' he pleaded, 'don't do this.'

'I have to. You leave me no choice.'

'And how will you ever explain it to the others? There are witnesses downstairs.'

'Witnesses who will find you fallen from the top landing.'

The shock hit William like a physical blow. 'You'd do that to me?' he gasped. 'Your own nephew?'

'Oh, don't worry, you'll be unconscious when I tip you over.'

'You think Toby will keep quiet? He already knows something is wrong.'

'Toby will watch his mouth or he'll suffer the same fate as you. He's no kin of mine. My real heir died at birth.'

With that Seth lunged forward and William reacted instinctively, pulling the skull from his pocket and lashing at Seth's face with the sharp beak, putting all his strength behind the blow. The skull splintered into fragments and Seth reeled aside with a shriek of pain, blood spraying from the wound. He tripped over the table and fell, scattering the other skulls in all directions. Before he even hit the floorboards, William was in motion, jumping over his prostrate form and then unlocking the door. He flung it wide and ran out onto the landing, realising even as he did so that he should have pulled out the key and secured the door from the outside. He was about to turn back when an angry bellow from within dissuaded him. Instead, he ran on along the landing, made it to the top of the staircase and started down, only to find that Toby was already halfway up, blocking his route.

'Hold on there, cousin!' he shouted. He looked at William and his gaze moved downwards to take in the hand that had held the bird's skull. William glanced down at it and saw that his fingers were liberally splashed with crimson.

'What the hell is going on?' cried Toby. 'What have you done to Seth?'

'He tried to kill me,' William told him.

'Why would he do that? And...what were you saying before? About my mother?'

Just then Seth came reeling out of the bedroom, blood pouring from a gash in the corner of his left eye. 'Hold him, Toby!' he shouted. 'The little whelp just attacked me.'

Toby moved obediently forward, his hands extended to make a grab, but William stopped him in his tracks with a few choice words: 'Toby, listen to me. Seth murdered your mother!'

Toby froze, his expression one of bewilderment. 'What?' he whispered. He snatched in a breath. 'What did you say?'

'Don't listen to him, Toby,' said Seth, mopping at his face with a silk handkerchief he had pulled from his pocket. 'The boy's a liar. You can surely see what he's capable of. Look what he just did to me.'

'*Think*, Toby,' insisted William. 'You know your mother's not just missing. She is dead. And you know she's not resting in peace.'

Toby shook his head. 'I don't—'

'And the quarry, Toby. Remember that. The rock falling. Do you really believe it was an accident?'

Seth had reached the top of the stairs now. 'Just hold him for me, Toby. I'll beat the truth out of him.'

Now Toby looked past William to his stepfather. 'But why would you do that?' he cried. 'To your own nephew?'

'Because . . . because he's an imposter. I don't even believe he *is* Matthew's son. I think he's just some workhouse child who found out about the percentage in the will and came here to try to worm his way into our family.'

'But . . . how could that be?' asked Toby. 'I thought . . . I thought you said there *was* no percentage?'

Seth looked dismayed. 'I mean . . . well, he must have thought . . . that he could get money out of me . . . somehow.' He pushed the bloody handkerchief into his pocket and started down the stairs, one hand outstretched to grab William's shoulder. 'You just leave him to me now. You go back downstairs and I'll get the answers out of him.'

William looked straight into Toby's eyes. 'Please,' he whispered. 'He plans to kill me too.'

A look passed across Toby's face then, a look of realisation. It was as though he had just woken from a deep sleep. He stepped quickly aside to let William pass. 'Go, cousin,' he said, and William dashed gratefully by him.

'No!' roared Seth. He made a last desperate lunge, but Toby turned to face him, barring his way. 'Toby, get out of the way! He'll escape!'

'Run, William,' shouted Toby. 'I'm just going to have a little talk with my stepfather.'

William needed no second bidding. He clattered down all three flights of stairs and didn't hesitate until he was on the ground floor. Then he headed for the kitchen and raced past a startled-looking Mrs Craddock, who was just bidding goodnight to Rhiannon.

'Where are you going?' yelled Mrs Craddock, but he ignored her. He sprinted past her, through the scullery and out of the back door. It was only once he was outside in the foggy night air that he realised there was only one place he could go now and he made straight for it, shouting for Idris as he ran. William didn't know how long Toby might delay Seth, but he thought it wouldn't be for more than a few minutes. Toby was sturdy but no match for his powerful stepfather.

Idris, alerted by his cries, met him at the open doorway. 'Will'yam!' he cried. 'What's wrong?'

'Saddle up Maggie,' cried William. 'Quickly. You've got to get me to Porthmadog, now!'

Idris stared at him blankly for a moment, then recognising the urgency spun around and ran back inside. William could hear the jangling of a harness as Idris hurried to get Maggie saddled up. William's only plan was to go for help in Porthmadog, find somebody who would listen to him. He remembered what Mr Cadwallader had told him: that Seth was friends with the police and had paid them handsomely to keep out of his affairs, so there was no point in going to *them*, but surely, William told himself, if he made for a public place and made enough noise, he could lead some people to the old chapel to show them what was hidden there. Then they'd have to believe him, wouldn't they? They'd *have* to help him. As he drew up his plan, he paced anxiously up and down, peering towards the house, now little more than a vague grey shape in the fog. 'Hurry, Idris!' he shouted, but there was no answer from within.

After what seemed an eternity, Idris led Maggie out into the open, and at the same moment William saw a tall figure striding towards him. Idris hadn't seen anything yet. He vaulted up into the saddle and reached out a hand for William to grasp.

'Idris!' Seth's voice was a roar that made Idris snatch the hand back again, as though he'd been scalded. 'Stay exactly where you are. Do *not* help the boy. Do you hear me? If you help him, I'll take my riding crop to you.'

Idris's face registered panic. 'Mr Jessop is angry!' he whimpered.

William gazed up at him. 'Idris,' he said, 'listen to me, not him.'

'Stay where you are!' bellowed Seth, striding closer. 'I'm warning you.'

Idris looked down at William. 'Mr Jessop says not to help Will'yam,' he whimpered. 'Mr Jessop bring out riding crop.'

'Idris, look at me. Listen!' William stared straight into Idris's eyes, realising that this was his last chance. 'Mr Jessop killed Mistress Audrina. Do you understand? He murdered her and buried her on the beach. Now... now he means to kill me too!'

A series of expressions passed across Idris's face. Confusion, sadness, disgust. And finally anger. His eyes blazed. He thrust the hand again, and when William took it, he swung him up onto the saddle, behind him.

There was a brief, exasperated yell from Seth, and then Idris kicked his bare heels into Maggie's flanks and they were off, heading for the gate.

CHAPTER TWENTY
PURSUIT

They galloped into the fog, and once again there was that weird sensation of not actually going anywhere. Idris had taken a track over the cliffs, one that William didn't recognise, but realised would eventually lead them down into Porthmadog. He clung on, thinking frantically as he did so.

He'd go to the Quarryman's Arms, he decided. Hopefully it would be full of workers, indulging in their nightly pastime of drinking ale. He'd run into the place, shouting as loudly as he could; he'd make sure that he involved everyone, because the more witnesses he had, the better his chance of survival. Seth couldn't harm him in front of so many people, could he? And William wouldn't delay. He'd lead whoever would go with him straight to the old chapel, because if too much time went by, Seth could easily ride over there and remove the casket. Right now it was the only piece of hard evidence William had.

Grey shapes flitted by them in the mist – the gaunt, skeletal outlines of trees, clawing at the heavens – and William was just beginning to think that they really did have a chance of getting away from Seth, when there was a sudden, long shriek from somewhere away to their left and something big flapped up into the sky. Whatever it was, it scared Maggie. She reared frantically, snorting in terror, and Idris's weight shifted abruptly backwards. William felt himself sliding and he tried desperately to cling on, but then he was out of the saddle and tumbling towards the snow-covered ground. The snow cushioned his fall, but an instant later Idris's flailing figure came down on top on him, driving the breath from his lungs. Maggie, still spooked, galloped away into the mist. William could hear her hoofbeats thudding away from them. He groaned, struggled into a sitting position and shook Idris. 'Are you all right?' he asked. 'Call Maggie back, quickly, we need to...'

He realised with a sinking feeling that Idris was unresponsive. He knelt beside him and turned him onto his back, saw a dark abrasion on his forehead where one of Maggie's hind hooves must have caught him a kick as he tumbled to the ground. 'Idris!' he hissed. 'Idris, please wake up!' William shook him hard, but though the man's chest was rising and falling, he was clearly out cold.

'Oh no!' William got to his feet and looked desperately around. What was he supposed to do *now*? He wasn't even sure in which direction Porthmadog lay. Just then he heard another long, ululating shriek from right above him, the sound of huge wings beating the air. He remembered the last time he'd heard that sound, the afternoon when they'd been returning from the quarry in the growler. And he remembered something that Rhiannon had told him. '*The* Gwrach *only comes when somebody is going to die...*'

A chill went through him that seemed to freeze the blood in his veins. He told himself he had to get moving. He'd send somebody back for Idris when he reached Porthmadog. But which way *was* it?

He started running in what he hoped was the right direction, but he'd only gone a short distance when he became aware of a soft sound behind him, the sound of padded feet crunching in the thick snow. He looked over his shoulder and nearly screamed aloud in sheer terror. Two sleek grey shapes were hurtling out of the fog towards him, their heads down, tongues lolling. The wolfhounds!

Somehow he managed to keep going, horribly aware that he had no chance of outrunning the dogs, but he'd be damned if he was going to give up without a fight. He kept thinking of the first time he'd seen them, how Seth had thrown them the remains of a chicken leg, how it had been snapped up in an instant by powerful jaws, and the thought of those sharp teeth closing around his own limbs filled him with absolute dread. He ran until the sound of their paws was almost upon him and then he turned, his fists raised to punch as the creatures closed on him.

But a curious thing happened. Both dogs stopped in their tracks and skidded to a silent, quivering halt, their eyes staring at William in mute shock – no, not at *him*, but at something behind him, something that seemed to terrify them. They began to back slowly away, their hackles raised, their teeth bared and they were whimpering like a pair of puppies. Then they turned and slunk away into the fog, their tails between their legs.

William twisted slowly around, full of dread himself, just in time to see Audrina turning away from him, her lantern raised. He realised that she must have been standing right behind him, staring down at the dogs.

As he gazed after her, she raised her free hand to beckon

to him to follow her. He hesitated for a moment. Was she showing him the way to Porthmadog? What if she was luring him into some kind of trap? But then he thought about Seth, who would surely be out looking for him by now, who must have set the dogs after him, and he saw no option but to throw caution aside and go after her, realising as he did so that she was leaving no footprints in the snow. Her figure kept slipping in and out of the mist ahead of him, but every time he thought he'd lost her, he soon caught sight of the faint pool of light from the lantern, floating along through the greyness like a beacon, so he kept following that, hoping against hope that soon he would see the road that led down into the valley. He walked for what felt like several minutes and then stopped in his tracks as he heard the distant sound of hoofbeats approaching. A riot of thoughts spilled through his head. Perhaps Idris had recovered and had found Maggie! Maybe he was ready to ride on to Porthmadog. Or... it was just Maggie. If that was the case, William would try grabbing hold of her bridle and do his best to ride her to Porthmadog himself.

He felt a momentary sense of elation as, sure enough, the shape of a horse loomed out of the mist – but the feeling evaporated instantly when he saw that this horse had a *rider*.

William stared open-mouthed in dismay as he recognised the horseman galloping towards him, a riding crop clutched in one hand.

'Ah, so there you are, nephew!' called Seth mockingly. 'Fancy meeting you out here in this wilderness! And what the hell did you do to my dogs? They fled past me yelping!'

William turned on his heels and ran once again, slipping and sliding in the snow, no longer knowing or caring where he was going, only convinced that he had to try to escape, that he couldn't just stop and face Seth. He looked desperately this way and that for the light of the lantern, but it was gone now, so he ran blindly into the fog, horribly aware of the sound of hoofbeats behind him, getting louder by the moment. An instant later Sabre swept by him and something lashed across his back, sending a jolt of pure agony through him. He stumbled, nearly fell, but somehow managed to stay upright. He changed direction and ran on again, while Seth reined Sabre to a halt and turned him around.

'It's useless!' Seth shouted. 'You can't outrun a horse, boy.'

William wasn't going to stop and debate the matter; he only knew he had to try. Again there was the sound of hoofbeats following him, drawing closer by the moment, and he steeled himself for another lash of the riding crop. At the last instant he ducked and switched direction, aware of the crop swishing through the air inches above his unprotected head. He kept going, knowing all too well that he couldn't keep this up for very much longer. His heart was already hammering in his chest, his breath coming in shallow gasps, as his eyes searched desperately for some kind of refuge.

And suddenly, amazingly, it loomed out of the fog, a circle of tall shapes, rearing up like giants on the deserted hilltop. The standing stones! Rhiannon had warned him they were something to avoid at all cost, the lair of the *Gwrach*, but it seemed to him now that they would at least provide him with a potential hiding place, a shield from that vicious crop. Without hesitating, he ran into the circle and put his back up against the nearest stone, while he struggled to recover his breath.

Seth slowed Sabre to a walk. 'Think you'll be safe in there?' he asked. He sounded amused. 'Clearly you don't know your history. That place has been a site of carnage for thousands of years.' He began to ride the horse slowly around the circumference of the circle, pausing occasionally to peer inside. 'This is just a waste of time, boy. You may as well come out and face the music. Don't worry, I'll make it quick for you. It'll be over in moments.'

William said nothing. He didn't want to give his position away. He peered around the edge of the stone and watched as Seth clicked his tongue and tried to turn Sabre into the circle, but the horse snorted and pulled back, unwilling to enter. 'Stupid brute,' growled Seth. He brought the riding crop down hard against the stallion's flanks, but the horse reared up, stamped his feet, his eyes rolling in their sockets. After a few moments, Seth cursed loudly and dismounted. He threw down the riding crop. Sabre turned and trotted away into the mist. Seth walked into the circle. William moved quickly around the stone to the front of it, but when he peered around the side, he could no longer see Seth, who had slipped into the drifting mist at the centre of the circle. Then Seth's disembodied voice spoke, sounding worryingly close by. 'You know, William, this is all such a waste,' he murmured. 'If you want to know the truth, there's something about you that I respect. If you'd only been clever enough to keep your nose out of my business, the two of us could actually have worked together.'

William looked helplessly around. He knew Seth was somewhere near, but he still couldn't see him. He didn't dare move from his position, in case Seth spotted him.

'Take Toby,' continued Seth, sounding surprisingly calm. 'He actually tried to stand up to me back at the house. The first time he's ever shown any backbone. But he just doesn't have it in him. For all his size, the lad's as soft as butter. One good punch and he went down like a sack of potatoes.' The voice was getting quieter now, as though Seth was moving further away around the circle. 'You, though, I dare say you'd have put up a better fight. Maybe that brother of mine taught you how to handle yourself. I wonder, did he do that? Gave you boxing lessons, did he?' A pause, as though Seth was waiting for an answer, but William knew it would be stupid to reply; it would only give his position away. 'Ah, you're not going to be fooled so easily, are you?' observed Seth. 'Which makes what I have to do now even more of a shame. If only we could have...'

His voice broke off in surprise as that terrifying sound rang out again, a shriek as though some giant eagle was soaring in the foggy air above them. 'You hear that?' asked Seth, after a few moments of silence. 'The *Gwrach* senses a death coming. She's come for *you*, boy. She's always there when somebody dies. You'd better prepare yourself.'

William felt a cold shudder go through him, but he stayed silent, not willing to give his uncle a clue as to where he was.

As he stood, his back up against stone, he became aware of something strange. It felt to him as if the hard surface against which he was pressed was beginning to vibrate, as though it was somehow coming alive.

'Let me see now, which stone are you hiding behind?' murmured Seth. 'This one? No...this one? No! Show yourself, cousin. I'm getting tired of this...'

William thought about chancing another run, telling himself that now Seth was without a horse, William had a much better chance of outpacing him. If he only knew in which direction Porthmadog lay! The problem was, he could just as easily find himself running back towards the house, which would be a disaster. Or, worse still, running off the edge of the cliff to his doom...But, he reasoned, if he stayed where he was, he would eventually be found, and that would be the end of him. So he steeled himself to make a last, desperate sprint for survival. He snatched in a breath and...

And then a hand came around the edge of the stone and grabbed him by his collar, yanked him away from cover and into the circle. 'There you are at last, nephew! I knew I'd find you sooner or later. Now then, no point in fighting it. You just come along with me...'

William kicked and struggled, tried lashing out with his fists, but Seth's grip was too powerful to resist. He dragged William to the very centre of the circle, where there lay a large stone slab. William was lifted into the air and flung down hard onto his back, the pain of the impact sending ripples of agony though his body. 'You know what this stone was for?' asked Seth, leaning over him. 'It's where the pagan priests used to make sacrifice to their gods. Of course, they were just ignorant heathens, but they understood one thing: when somebody opposes you, it's best to make a quick end of them.'

William tried to struggle upright, but Seth's gloved hand slapped him hard across the face, knocking him flat, making his senses spin. Now Seth leaned over him and clamped both hands around the boy's throat. 'Goodbye, William,' he said, and his expression was one of genuine regret. 'I'm sorry it has to end this way.'

The hands tightened their grip, cutting off William's air supply. He stared imploringly up at his uncle, but saw no mercy in the man's dark eyes, just a cold, relentless glare. A bright red mist seemed to fill William's head, his senses began to swim and he realised there was no hope for him now... no hope at all... He told himself that soon he would see his father and all his struggles would be over... but then he became aware of something puzzling, something that gave him a tiny spark of hope.

A light. A yellow glow. It was floating in the air behind Seth, and gliding steadily closer. William stared in disbelief as a cloaked figure drifted out of the fog behind Seth, carrying her lantern, the cowled unseen face looking intently at his back. And then a low voice said, 'Seth.'

At the sound of his name, Seth released his grip on William and twisted around in surprise. William coughed and spluttered, and managed to roll off the stone and onto the ground. He lay there on his side, gasping for breath, looking at the scene in front of him in amazement.

Audrina stood in front of Seth, her lantern illuminating his astonished expression.

'No,' he whispered. 'No. This cannot be.'

She didn't say anything for quite a while. She just let out a long sigh. It sounded to William like the weariest sigh that anybody had ever made. And then she said one word, in a deep whisper: 'Murderer!'

Seth shook his head. 'Please,' he whispered, 'Audrina, I'm...I'm sorry.'

She shook her head and repeated the word, louder now, almost a shout of anger. 'MURDERER!'

'You must understand,' whispered Seth, 'and have mercy on me. I...didn't mean to kill you. You have to believe me. I lashed out. It was...an accident.' A silence. 'I...I haven't spent a penny of your inheritance. I have lived like a hermit...a pauper. You must be merciful!'

She said nothing – she just tilted back her head and looked to the heavens. Puzzled, Seth tried to see what she was looking at, and William too felt compelled to follow their example. There was a long silence, a silence so deep that William felt that it might go on for ever.

And then, with heart-stopping suddenness, something came plummeting down from above – a thin, wiry corpse-like thing, wrapped in rags, powering through the air on great leathery wings. William saw her only for an instant, but in perfect detail: the hideous wasted features, the black teeth, the lolling serpentine tongue. Seth had time for one scream of pure terror and then the *Gwrach*'s withered arms were around him, the black wings flapped and the creature lifted him kicking and struggling from the ground and upwards, into the night air. For an instant William saw the shape of the two figures as they ascended, and then the fog enfolded them like a blanket and there was one last helpless cry of horror from Seth, before silence returned.

A long moment followed, when nothing happened, when a strange all-enveloping peace prevailed. Then the cloaked figure turned to look down at William and the glow from the lantern illuminated Audrina's features, revealing them to him for the first time. If he had expected to see something horrifying, he was thankfully wrong. The face that smiled down at him was beautiful, the eyes a deep blue, the delicate nose perfectly shaped, the mouth a full pink cupid's bow. She nodded, as though offering him her thanks, and he realised that she had always needed Seth to be in this circle before she could take her vengeance. Suddenly it all made sense to him. The animal skulls arranged into a perfect circle on the table, the rings drawn in the frost on the dormer window and the words *Bring him*, even the time that he had seen her standing in the centre of these very stones, beckoning to him. There must have been something about the circle that gave her power, maybe something to do with the strange vibration he had felt in the stone. As William watched, she turned and, still carrying the lantern, walked calmly out of the circle and away into the banks of shifting grey fog. For a few moments he saw the dwindling light and then it was gone.

William staggered to his feet, using the flat stone to help

himself up. He coughed to clear his bruised throat. He lifted his head to look towards the sky, but there was silence there now, nothing to indicate where the *Gwrach* might have taken Seth, but William was fairly sure his uncle wouldn't be coming back any time soon.

Just then he became aware of someone emerging from the fog: a tall, gangling figure leading a horse by its reins, one hand pressed against his forehead.

'Idris?' croaked William. 'Is that you?'

'Will'yam!' Idris led Maggie closer, but stopped just outside the circle, looking nervously around. Maggie was flaring her nostrils and stamping her feet, close to panic again. 'This is a bad place,' said Idris. 'You should not be in there.' He dropped his hand to reveal the mark on his forehead and then he winced. 'Idris was knocked out,' he said. 'When he wakes up, Maggie is there, but no Will'yam.' He eased Maggie back from the edge of the stones and she quietened down a little.

'I . . . I was trying to get to Porthmadog on foot,' rasped William, 'but then I found myself here.'

'You come out,' said Idris, beckoning. 'Bad place. Everyone says so.'

William didn't need telling a second time. He stumbled out

of the circle and went to stand beside Maggie, leaning against her warm flank until the dizziness in his head subsided.

'We can ride now,' Idris assured him. 'We can go to Porthmadog for help.' He clambered back up into the saddle, with a little less dexterity than usual, and then reached down a hand to William, to help him up behind him. But once seated, William put a hand on Idris's shoulder. 'No,' he said. 'We shan't go to Porthmadog now. There's no need.'

'Where then?' asked Idris, surprised, turning to look at him.

'Home,' said William, and then he smiled, as he realised it was the first time he'd ever used that word to describe Jessop Rise.

'But ... what about Mr Jessop?' asked Idris.

'Oh, I don't think we need worry about him. Come on, let's head back.'

Idris was clearly puzzled, but he wheeled Maggie around, dug his heels into her flanks and started her on her way. After they had gone a short distance William glanced back for a final look at the standing stones, but they were already lost in the fog.

EPILOGUE
APRIL 1854

It was spring and Jessop Rise seemed a completely different place in the warm sunshine. The big house bustled with servants, overseen by Mrs Craddock, who as housekeeper now commanded a sizable staff: a cook, a couple of footmen and a house boy, as well as Rhiannon, who had insisted on retaining her post, even though she'd been offered the more prestigious one of housemaid. William had also offered her the chance to go back to school if she preferred, but she had politely declined, saying that she would much rather be at work, a decision that he had eventually accepted.

Out in the grounds, a team of gardeners was gradually getting the flowerbeds back into shape. And in the stables Idris now had a brand-new uniform, one that had actually been made to fit him. What's more, he was allowed to wear it whenever he wanted.

The young lawyer who called that day, a Mr Tennyson, was a different sort of fellow to Mr Cadwallader, younger and more intense, but he seemed efficient enough. He confessed that he'd only been at Thomas, Jenkins and Hughes a few weeks, a replacement for the late Mr Cadwallader. Toby and William met him in the dining room. It was warm enough not to have to bother with a fire, and there were no wolfhounds stretched out in front of the hearth. Toby had given them to a farmer who lived nearby. He admitted to William that he had never really liked them.

Mr Tennyson studied the copy document he had in front of him and then indicated the places on the original where the two cousins should sign their names. Toby lifted the pen first, but Mr Tennyson told him to wait a moment. 'You're absolutely sure about this?' he murmured. 'After all, the original bequest *was* for William to have only ten per cent of the quarry.'

Toby grinned. William noticed the slight scar above his right eye where Seth had punched him to the ground, still visible, even after more than three months. 'The house and the Ransome estate shall be mine,' said Toby. 'The quarry and all matters pertaining to it shall go to William,' he declared. 'And he'll inherit at eighteen, not twenty-one, just as soon as he's finished his schooling. That's all set out in here?'

Mr Tennyson nodded. 'It's a most unusual arrangement,' he said, 'and there were a few problems getting it approved, but it is all there, just as you instructed.'

'Good.' Toby signed his name with a flourish and then slid the papers over to William. 'And there are going to be some changes,' he said. 'William has informed me that he doesn't intend to run the quarry as my stepfather did. He's going to give his workers a much fairer deal.'

Mr Tennyson nodded. 'That's most commendable,' he said. 'I must say, it's very unusual for such a young man to be handed a business like this one, but . . . well, Toby, your grandparents felt that you were mature enough to act as guarantor on the matter, so . . . everything has been arranged accordingly.' He looked at William. 'You appreciate that, until you come of age, Toby will be *your* guarantor and you will have to defer to him, should you happen to disagree regarding any aspect of the business.'

William nodded. He and Toby got along very well these days, so he couldn't imagine that there'd be a problem.

'Such a tragedy, what happened,' observed Mr Tennyson.

He was, of course, referring to a lot of things: the murder of Mr Cadwallader and his coachman, the discovery of the baby's body in the ruined chapel, the exhumation of Audrina's corpse in the spot on the beach that William had identified as her grave, and of course Seth's 'suicide'. His body had been found at the base of the cliffs a mile or so down the coast, a couple of days after the *Gwrach* had taken him. His injuries indicated that he must have fallen from a great height indeed. The subsequent inquest ruled that he had taken his own life while the balance of his mind was disturbed, and William had decided not to correct that assumption. He doubted that people were quite ready to hear the truth of what had really happened that night, even though he was happy for them to know that his uncle had been a murderer and an adulterer. He had told Toby everything, of course. The young man had listened with mounting amazement, but hadn't challenged one detail. After that, the two of them had never spoken of the matter again.

It was interesting to note that after the ensuing scandal there were only a very few people willing to attend Seth's funeral. Interestingly, the chief law officer of the county wasn't one of them, probably because his dealings with Seth

Jessop were currently under investigation for corruption. William had hoped that there might be one uninvited visitor to the interment. As the coffin was lowered into the unconsecrated ground on the far side of the graveyard wall, an area reserved for those who had died by their own hand, William found himself looking expectantly around in the hope of glimpsing a hooded figure watching the proceedings. But there was nobody else, just the blank-faced, black-garbed mourners gathered around the open grave. William hadn't seen Audrina since the night of the stone circle and he felt strangely bereft that this was the case. He would have liked to see her again; he felt that he owed her so much.

He took the pen he was offered and inked his name onto the document, the one that would make him a rich man, the owner of Jessop Quarry. He had great plans for the place. It would continue to be a hive of industry but, he was determined, it would no longer be the hellhole that Seth Jessop had made it. It would be a place where men were pleased to work because they would receive a fair wage for a fair day's labour, a place where any man injured would be properly compensated. He was determined that none of his employees would ever go hungry or lose their homes. He knew that he had enough money to make all that a reality.

It was simply a case of taking less profit for himself. And he would be going back to school – possibly even on to university, in order to pursue his dream of one day becoming a doctor – leaving the day-to-day running of the quarry in the capable hands of Rhiannon's father, Huw. Toby, he knew, was planning to travel. He was already drawing up a list of places he wanted to visit. He would be taking plenty of notebooks with him, because he intended to write about his experiences.

'So,' said Mr Tennyson, taking the signed documents and slipping them into his briefcase, 'that appears to be everything. You are now officially the new owners of Ransome Rise –' he smiled at Toby – 'and Jessop Quarry.' He nodded to William. 'It only remains for me to wish you every success for the future.' He reached across the table and shook hands with them both.

'Thank you,' said Toby. 'We'll show you out, shall we?'

The two of them accompanied the young lawyer out of the dining room and along the hallway, where decorators were applying fresh paper to the walls, ready for Toby's grandparents, who would be moving in later that month. William was to have a chamber on the second floor, right next to Audrina's old room, which at Toby's insistence was to be kept exactly as it was. From the kitchen came the clatter of workmen, who were replacing the soot-blackened oven with a brand-new model, under the watchful eye of a delighted Mrs Craddock.

'My goodness, you really are changing the old place, aren't you?' observed Mr Tennyson.

'My stepfather ran a cold house,' said Toby. 'My plan is to make it a warm one. Somewhere that people will actually want to visit.'

'I wonder what Mr Jessop would make of all this industry,' murmured Mr Tennyson.

'I expect he'll be spinning in his grave,' said Toby, and William had to stifle a laugh.

A houseboy opened the front door and the three of them sauntered out onto the drive, where Mr Tennyson's coach was waiting for him.

William had a disturbing vision of that fateful night when Mr Cadwallader had driven away from the house. 'Tell your coachman to be careful going over the rise,' he said. 'It's quite tricky there.'

Mr Tennyson raised his eyebrows. 'I take your point,' he said. 'We'll proceed with the utmost caution.' He shook hands with both of them and then climbed into the coach.

He leaned out of the window. 'A word of advice,' he said. 'You're two rich young men now. Great wealth can spoil things for some people. I would suggest that you consider what is important and spend every penny wisely.'

'We intend to,' Toby assured him. 'Thank you, sir.'

The coachman clucked his tongue and the horses started forward, pulling the coach towards the gates. They watched until it had turned onto the clifftop road.

'Well, I'm heading inside,' announced Toby. 'I'm going to have another crack at that opening chapter.' He had recently started trying to write a detective novel and had quickly discovered that it wasn't anything like as easy as he had anticipated. 'You coming?' he asked.

'No, I think I'll enjoy the sun for a while,' said William. 'It seems a very long time since I saw any.'

The two young men studied each other in silence for a moment. William knew that they would never be alike, but he was certain that they would be able to get along together without any trouble. They had a mutual respect, and, in the end he supposed that was what mattered most.

'I'll see you later, cousin,' said Toby. He turned and strode back towards the house and in through the front door.

William gazed off towards the entrance gates. Beyond it,

the clifftops were thick with wild flowers and the sky a deep China blue. It seemed like a different place entirely. He slipped his hands into his pockets and wandered along the drive and out through the gates.

It only took him a short time to find the place where a steep track led straight down to the beach. He descended and walked across the flat stretch of sand until he came to the spot where Audrina's remains had been discovered. Her body had been disinterred and reburied in the Ransome family vault in Porthmadog, but a simple bronze cross had been added to the flat top of the long black stone, only a few days earlier, with her name inscribed on it, together with the years of her birth and death. It had been Toby's idea, something to mark the spot. There was still a selection of flowers and posies arranged around the base of the cross, where the villagers had paid their last respects. William stood looking down in silence for a moment and then he glanced around, wanting to be sure that there was nobody within hearing.

'I wanted to thank you,' he said. 'For everything you did for me.'

He hesitated, listening intently, but all he could hear was the cawing of gulls and the restless rush of the sea pounding on the shore. He thought for a moment, wanting to find the right words. He knew her body was no longer here, but something told him that her spirit still might be.

'And... I wanted to say... if you ever need help again, don't be afraid to come and find me. You know where I'll be.'

Again he waited, but still there was nothing. He sighed and said, 'Well, goodbye, Audrina. I'll visit you again soon.'

He turned and started walking along the path that led up to the Rise. Halfway there, something made him stop and look over his shoulder. She was standing beside the memorial, cloaked as ever, watching him intently. He was too far away to see the expression on her face. He smiled and lifted a hand to wave, but he got no reaction from her. Even so, it made him happy to think that she was still out there, watching him.

He turned away again and walked back to the house, humming a half-remembered tune.

THE PIPER

Winner of the Scottish Children's Book Award

DANNY WESTON

He who pays the piper calls the tune

On the eve of World War Two, Peter and Daisy are evacuated to a remote farmhouse. From the moment they arrive, they are aware that something evil haunts the place. Who plays the eerie music that can only be heard at night? And why is Daisy so irresistibly drawn to it? When Peter uncovers a dark family secret, he begins to realise that his sister is in terrible danger, and to save her he must face an ancient curse...

'Wonderfully twisty chiller that's sure to make you want to keep all of the lights on'
Scotsman

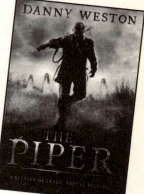

9781783440511 £7.99

DANNY WESTON

You'll do whatever he tells you

Owen lives with his cruel aunt in her small seaside guesthouse, and he's desperate to escape his life of drudgery. Then he meets a mysterious ventriloquist whose dummy, Mr Sparks, really seems able to speak by himself. And Mr Sparks is looking for a new, much younger assistant, someone who can help him run away from the dark secrets of the past.

This could be the answer to Owen's problems. But just who is controlling who?

9781783443215 £7.99

HAUNTED

A FANTASTIC COLLECTION OF GHOST STORIES FROM TODAY'S LEADING CHILDREN'S AUTHORS

'A chilling slice of horror. An excellent balance of traditional and modern and a perfect pocket-money purchase for winter evenings.' *Daily Mail*

Derek Landy, Philip Reeve, Joseph Delaney, Susan Cooper, Eleanor Updale, Jamila Gavin, Mal Peet, Matt Haig, Berlie Doherty, Robin Jarvis and Sam Llewellyn have come together to bring you eleven ghost stories: from a ghost walk around York; to a drowned boy, who's determined to find someone to play with; to a lost child trapped in a mirror, ready to pull you in; to devilish creatures, waiting with bated breath for their next young victim; to an ancient woodland reawakened. Some will make you scream, some will make you shiver, but all will haunt you gently long after you've put the book down.

9781849393218 £6.99

NIGHT ON TERROR ISLAND

It's the scariest movie ever and they're stuck in it!

PHILIP CAVENEY

Have you ever wanted to be in the movies?

Kip has, and when he meets mysterious Mr Lazarus he thinks his dream's come true. Because Mr Lazarus can project people into movies! Films like *Terror Island*, full of hungry sabre-toothed tigers and killer Neanderthals.

When you're in a film, everything is real: real bullets, real swords, real monsters. But beware . . . if you don't get out by the time the closing credits roll, you'll be trapped in the film forever!

Can Kip rescue his sister before the sabre-toothed tigers get her? And if he can — how is he going to get back?!

9781849392709 £6.99